Lexington Historical Society

Proceedings of Lexington Historical Society

and papers relating to the history of the town - Vol. 4

.

.

Lexington Historical Society

Proceedings of Lexington Historical Society
and papers relating to the history of the town - Vol. 4

ISBN/EAN: 9783337221324

Printed in Europe, USA, Canada, Australia, Japan

Cover: Foto ©Andreas Hilbeck / pixelio.de

More available books at **www.hansebooks.com**

FIRST PARISH CHURCH

PROCEEDINGS

OF THE

LEXINGTON HISTORICAL SOCIETY

WITH SOME OF THE PAPERS
READ AT ITS MEETINGS

VOL. IV

[1905-1910]

LEXINGTON, MASSACHUSETTS
PUBLISHED BY THE SOCIETY
1912

CONTENTS.

THE EARLY SCHOOLS OF LEXINGTON.

By Alonzo E. Locke. Read December 10, 1889.

As the old town records have been about the only source from which I could draw in making up this paper, it necessarily becomes, to a great extent, simply a collection of dates and names; but, as I cannot find that the numerous entries appearing on the records concerning the early schools have ever been brought together in a concise manner, I have considered it well to put them in the form of this paper for future reference.

Starting with the building of the first school-house in 1714, I have come down to 1804, at which time the school-houses were located in and served much the same territory as the schools of to-day. It is exceedingly interesting to note the changes in the character and number of the schools, and it is certainly creditable to the town that it was ever ready to sustain as good schools as the times demanded and it could consistently afford.

The first record we find concerning a school or school-house for our town was made November 2, 1714, when the town "Voted to *Eract* a schoolhouse 28 ft. long, 20 ft. wide, and 8 or 9 foot stud and that it be placed on land purchased of Muzzey,"—referring to the Common. In this connection I would state that the land for the Common was purchased at two different times. In 1711 one and one-half acres were bought, and in 1721 another acre was secured, giving the present area of our Common.

The timber for this first school-house was taken from the town's lands,—the ministerial lands, probably. The building was placed near the site of the monument, evidently; for later on, in the town reports, this part of the

Common is spoken of as School-house Hill. Nothing is said in the records as to the completion of the school-house, but it was voted on August 29, 1715, "That the Town will have a school and to chose a committee to secure a teacher that will meet the law."

But not till the next year did the town vote to provide money for the school. May 19, 1716, the following comprehensive vote was passed: "Voted £15 for school. Also that all scholars that come to school paie 2 pens per week for reading, 3 pens for wrighting and siphering and what that amounts to at the end of the year so much of the £15 to be deducted and stopped in the Town Treasury whilst the next year and that a committee provide a school master as the law directs."

With such spelling and such manner of expression, surely the town clerk himself should have contributed his pence and attempted the mastery of spelling.

It does not appear that the school was opened until about November 1, 1716; for the selectmen on March 18, 1717, resolved to pay Captain Joseph Estabrook £15 for five months, ending the last of March, 1717.

Joseph Estabrook, Lexington's first schoolmaster, was a brother of Rev. Benjamin Estabrook, Lexington's first minister. They were sons of Rev. Joseph Estabrook of Concord.

In May, 1717, the selectmen voted to establish female schools,—that is, for girls and young children,—one in the north and one in the south part of the town. At this time, it must be remembered, there were few houses in the village.

May, 1718, the town voted that five female schools be set up, one at the centre, the others as convenient.

There was but one school building,—that in the village,— and in the town records this is spoken of as "the school-house." The district schools were held at different houses, the people of the district furnishing the room. A Mrs. Clapp taught in the school-house in the summer of 1718, but Captain Estabrook had taught during the previous winter.

May 17, 1719, the town "voted to have a school kept in town the full year, a moving school, to be kept a quarter of a year in a place"; but the next town meeting rescinded the vote, and school was kept the whole year in the school-house.

The selectmen at this time agreed with Sir John Hancock to keep the school for £40.

On September 12, 1720, it was voted to have a grammar school five months in the year. Captain Estabrook again keeps the school, as he did also the next year, 1721. Nothing is said of the schools in the outskirts of the town.

On May 17, 1722, £25 was voted for schools, and female schools were kept in two places, but none in the village.

August 17, 1723, £25 for grammar school in school-house.

May 14, 1724, £25 was voted for a grammar school at the school-house, each scholar to pay four pence per week. Captain Estabrook was still teaching, but in last quarter of 1724 John Sparhawk's name appears.

Although the town voted in 1724 to have a grammar school, it is evident that the selectmen did not carry out the vote, for the town is complained of to the Court for not having a grammar school.

About this time John Bowman kept the school. He lived on the old road leading from Arlington Heights to Watertown Street, the road from East Lexington to Waverley (the old house is now standing).* Later he married a daughter of Parson Hancock, and became a minister and a very prominent man of Dorchester.

* It was destroyed by fire April 1, 1905.

At this time various sums were spent by the town in repairing the school-house.

Up to this time, scholars had paid for their instruction, but in May, 1726, the town voted to provide "Free Schools." In 1728 it was "voted to have a running school, in the school-house and four quarters of the town, and that the above school should move once a month." £45 was voted.

July of this year "it was agreed with Rev. John Hancock"—the "present minister," as the record says— "that his son Ebenezer should teach the grammar" (at which, by the way, Latin was taught) "and English school for £40 for the year next ensuing."

This year the town is divided into five parts: 1st, Centre; 2d, South-easterly (East Lexington); 3d, South-westerly (Waltham); 4th, North-westerly (Concord Hill); 5th, North-easterly (North Lexington). "Thirty one days in each at a time and go around twice."

In 1729 Mr. Hancock kept a moving school.

In 1730 the school-house and meeting-house were repaired, and in 1731 it is noted that Mr. Hancock is still the teacher.

The town voted in May, 1732, "to have a well dug and stoned for use of school and town people on Sabbath days to drink at, the well to have a curb and sweep to draw water," and later on we find that the well cost £5 19s.

Mr. Hancock continues to teach through 1732, and in 1733 he is to be given £36 for nine months, having Saturdays to himself.

During this year (1733) he becomes his father's colleague, and is paid £200 as pastor and school-teacher. The selectmen were requested by the town to see if Mr. Hancock would take Latin scholars in summer.

There are few entries for the next three or four years.

In 1734 the turret on the school-house was completed, and in 1735 the chimney and underpinning needed attention. Joseph Brown, Mr. Phillips, and William Jennison were teachers in 1736 and 1737. In December, 1737, William Fessenden was selected, to be paid £45 for nine months, the selectmen to pay for his "entertainment" (that is, his board) above ten shillings per week.

In 1738 a moving school was tried again, and, if any corner of the town failed to provide a place for the school and a boarding-place for the teacher, the school was kept at the school-house.

A curious entry in this latter year is noted in the records, for it seems the town warned the Irish, then only four in number, out of the town.

Josiah Pearce was chosen teacher for £80 per year,—currency was depreciating in value,—but the selectmen agreed with him that he was "to be freed if he can have a better employment if he gives a months warning." Evidently he did not get a better position, for he was still teaching in 1741, although Jonathan Hoar taught for one quarter in 1740.

Matthew Bridge, Jr., received £80 for nine months, in 1741, for keeping a grammar and English school, and continued through 1742. In this year a contribution was taken up for his benefit,—probably in the church,—as the records say, "by reason of his giving so unusually dear for his board."

In 1742 Jonathan Townsend taught for £90.

In 1742, 1743, and 1744 schools were kept in five "quarters" of the town and at the centre. In 1744 the town voted that for each child attending the grammar school two feet of wood must be sent. Nathaniel Trask was the teacher this year and in 1745.

In 1746 Evard Holyoke was the master, and Rev. Timothy Harrington was engaged for 1747 for £75, old tenor, equal to £25 good money. This was the compact made with him:—

"School to be dismissed on all Public Occasions, and if time should be lost should be taken out of his salary. Five hours in winter and six afterwards."

In 1747 to 1748 Mr. Harrington retained his place, teaching from July to May for £130,—the currency was further depreciated,—and boarding himself. He was this year to have "Lecture days in town; one-half a day at funerals; at raisings; at ordinations in the neighborhood. Training days to be respected as h-o-l-y-days." At this time, 1747–48, girls, or rather g-a-i-r-l-s, were to be admitted to the grammar school for the first time.

John Fowle, it seems, finished out Mr. Harrington's year, and he was to admit "gairls" to his school and enjoy the same privileges as to "holydays." It was agreed with John Muzzey to board him for £1 15s. per week, while Deacon Stone was to find him in candles at 5s. per pound.

The town shifts back and forth from 1749 to 1758, first moving about the four or five quarters of the town, only to come back for a time to the school-house. Two years of this period Nathaniel Robbins acted as master, having the privilege to preach one-half day a week "anywhere."

Stephen Coolidge next presided over the schools, but no mention is made of his salary or of favors granted him.

Lieutenant Josiah Parker was paid 4s., so the records tell us, for a great chair for the school-house.

In January, 1758, Mr. Whittemore teaches in four quarters of the town.

In 1759 the school-house boasts of having a table provided.

For the next three years the school jumps about as usual, under the care of Josiah Bridge and Timothy Fuller.

On May 17, 1761, is recorded quite an extensive vote, as follows: "To keep writing or women schools in outskirts of Town, but no person living within one and one half miles of the schoolhouse to have the benefit of the writ-

ing school." "Voted to build a new schoolhouse where
old one stands and appoint a committee to build. To
sell the old schoolhouse and take timber for new one from
the ministerial lands. The schoolhouse to be 20 ft. square
and 6 1-2 feet between floors."

While this house was being erected, Widow Harrington
was paid 5s. 4d. for the use of her house, and Daniel Leeds
wielded the rod. The new building cost £43 13s. 6d. 1f.

Peter Whitney's name appears in 1762, and Joseph
Brown's in 1763, William Bowen being the next teacher
mentioned, in 1770. The schools were conducted as in
previous years, though we find that in 1765 there were
six "quarters" in the town. Oliver Wellington Lane was
master in 1772.

The town in May, 1773, "Voted seven squadrons for
women's schools." The town clerk evidently meant
that the town should be divided into seven "quarters."
We have previously had four, five, and six quarters, and
to accomplish such a division would puzzle, I think, some
of our school-children of this day.

We are now coming to an interesting period, and on
May 29, 1775, the town voted that no grammar school be
kept on account of "the present heavy charges"; but,
nevertheless, there were provided women's schools for
the children, and with commendable generosity the town
said they should be free.

Nothing of interest is recorded for the next few years,
except the names of the teachers.

It was in 1781 that the currency was of so little real
value that it is said that it took £80 of it to equal £1 of
good money.

In 1784 Benjamin Green was the teacher, and he boarded
in the family of Rev. Mr. Clarke and married one of his
daughters. Mr. Green afterward became, in turn, a
minister, lawyer, judge, and was quite a noted man of his
time.

Then in 1786 followed Thaddeus Fisk, who married another of Rev. Mr. Clarke's daughters. Now accounts were kept in dollars, and Mr. Fisk was paid by the town $10 per week.

Rufus Merriam is mentioned in 1788, and Mr. Pitt Clark, A.B., in 1790. In this latter year, mention is made that Benjamin Phinney supplies a school-room for three months.

Mr. Pipon and Abiel Abbott taught in 1791, $9 per week being paid the latter.

In 1793 it was "Voted to have no grammar school in the schoolhouse, but to have a grammar school in each section of the Town."

This was followed by a vote in May, 1796, to build three school-houses. These were completed and first occupied in this year, 1796. The East School was situated on Mason's Hill, just below the Munroe Tavern; the South-west School, towards Waltham; and the North School, at North Lexington. It is further recorded that stoves were put up in these new buildings.

The old school at the centre was sold to Matthew Kelly for $48.50.

May 1, 1797, mention is made of the fact that a monument is to be placed on School-house Hill.

The town in 1800 voted that teachers must bring certificates of their qualifications and the selectmen must visit the school.

Then in June, 1804, there was passed a vote authorizing more school buildings,—one in the Scotland District, 23 by 18, one at *Smiths End*, 23 by 18, and one at the Centre, 28 by 22. This latter house stood forty feet west of the monument. The school-houses already established were to be moved to convenient places. Thus we find the schools arranged so that they served much the same sections of the town as are covered by the schools of to-day.

Some of our older citizens went to school in the house built at the centre in 1804, and I trust that some of them can give to the Historical Society many of their recollections, which would be thoroughly appreciated. From what I have been fortunate enough to hear, the boys, and girls, too, of that time, were up to their pranks when not mastering their "three R's," and the teachers were sorely taxed in their endeavors to keep strict discipline.

THE BATTLE OF LEXINGTON IN ENGLAND.

By Rev. C. A. Staples. Read October 11, 1898.

Immediately after the battle of Lexington the Provincial Congress of Massachusetts, in session at Watertown, took steps to have an account of that event transmitted to England. It was considered desirable that the American view of the events of April 19 should be spread before the English people in advance of the report of General Gage, which would, naturally, be most favorable to the cause of the king, throwing all blame upon our people. It was accordingly ordered that depositions be taken, at Lexington and Concord, of those engaged in the affair, as to what really transpired, and a committee was appointed to draw up an account for transmission to England. The depositions were taken, the account was prepared, a vessel was chartered, and Captain Richard Derby sailed from Salem for London, bearing the documents which he was to deliver to Mr. Arthur Lee, the agent of the Massachusetts Province in England. After a prosperous voyage Captain Derby reached London eleven days before the arrival of General Gage's despatches, which had been sent four days earlier than his. The news brought by Captain Derby was immediately published in the London papers and sent into every part of England, Scotland, and Ireland, and the original documents deposited with the mayor of London in Guildhall. It caused intense excitement. The government refused to credit it. It was declared impossible that British soldiers, the best-trained and best-armed troops in the world, had retreated before a rabble of undisciplined peasantry. No such intelligence had been received at the War Depart-

ment, and people were advised to await despatches from
General Gage before accepting such an improbable story.
To this Lee replied that the depositions could be seen at
Guildhall. "Read them," he said, "and judge if they
be true or false." The friends of America in England
were hardly less incredulous.

It seemed improbable that the patriots should have
sprung to arms at once, in such numbers and in a spirit
so firm and heroic as to put to flight a battalion of a thousand British soldiers, killing, wounding, and capturing
more than one-fourth of their number. But, after eleven
days of doubt and perplexity, General Gage's despatches
arrived, confirming those of the Provincial Congress in
almost every particular. There was no longer room for
unbelief. A sad and awful event had occurred, covering
the British arms with disgrace and opening a breach
which might never be healed. The Provincials had not
proved the cowards they had been called. They had not
run like sheep at the first appearance of the king's troops.
They were as brave and stubborn in defence of what they
believed to be their rights as the stoutest English hearts.

Such was the lesson which thoughtful and candid Englishmen drew from the battle of Lexington and the events
of the 19th of April, 1775. Convinced of the truth of the
reports and realizing the seriousness of the situation, a
meeting, at which the mayor presided, was held in London by the friends of America, to protest against the course
pursued by the government. A petition was presented
to the king, beseeching him to dismiss his ministers whose
harsh and unjust course had brought this disaster upon
the country and was alienating His Majesty's loyal subjects, and to adopt a more conciliatory policy. The petition proved useless. The ministers, upon whom the
responsibility legally rested, were only carrying out the
policy of their master, George III., who believed in

the divine right of kings, and determined that these contu-
macious Yankees should be brought to respect and obey
his will. It was a sad, anxious time with the friends of
America in England. The patriots had many sympa-
thizers in the mother country, who believed the cause
was the cause of justice and freedom. Their leaders
boldly maintained it in Parliament, and the liberal press
went so far in condemning the policy of the government
and sustaining the American cause as to bring down upon
the editors heavy fines and imprisonment. The leading
liberal statesmen of England, alarmed at the impending
crisis, denounced the conduct of General Gage in sending
out the expedition to Lexington as most unwise and criminal. The firing upon the Provincials was nothing less
than cold-blooded murder, unjustified by any provocation. Such was the language freely used in private and,
sometimes, on the floor of Parliament, and published in
the London *Morning Chronicle*, subjecting the proprietor
to a suit for libel of the government. So seriously did the
father of the poet Rogers regard the news of the battle
of Lexington, and so deeply did he lay these unprovoked
murders to heart, that he caused the members of his family
to wear mourning as an expression of his sorrow and his
sympathy for the cruelly wronged American people.

In London at this time there existed an organization
called the Society of the Bill of Rights, or the Constitutional Society, formed, probably, to secure some more
liberal laws and an extension of the principles of popular
government. At a meeting of this society, held soon after
the news of the battle of Lexington had been received, the
unfortunate occurrence was warmly discussed and the conduct of the government severely condemned. One of the
members, Mr. John Horne, a clergyman of the Church of
England, settled in Kent, proposed that a subscription be
opened then and there, "for the benefit of the orphans,

aged parents and widows of our brethren murdered by the
King's troops at or near Lexington and Concord on the
19th of April, 1775." The proposition was adopted, and
contributions were then received to the fund. But Horne
went still farther. He drew up and printed in the *Morning
Chronicle* and London *Advertiser* a circular letter to the
friends of America, soliciting contributions to this fund.
In this letter he speaks of the men who fell at Lexington
and Concord as "our beloved American fellow-subjects
who, faithful to the character of Englishmen, preferring
death to slavery, were, for that reason only, inhumanly
murdered by the King's troops in the province of Massachusetts on the 19th of April, 1775." The appeal was
successful, and the sum of £100, equivalent to more than
$1,000 in the money of our day, was raised and sent to Dr.
Franklin, who had then returned to America, the same to
be used to relieve the suffering and distress caused by the
ruthless slaughter of men standing up for their rights as
free-born Englishmen. This bold proceeding gave great
offence to the government, and was regarded as a chal-
lenge to the ministers to contest the statements made in the
circular or to prosecute Horne. The printer was arrested
and convicted of publishing a libel on the government.
Then an action was brought by the attorney-general
against Horne for "contempt," as he says, "of our Lord
and King in open violation of the laws of this kingdom,
to the evil and pernicious example of all others in like cases
offending and against the peace and dignity of our Sovereign Lord the King." Then follow the specific charges
already given,—the writing and publishing of the circular
and the raising of the money remitted to Dr. Franklin.
Horne was put under bonds to appear when the case should
be called, which for some reason did not occur till the
autumn of 1777, when the case was tried before a jury,
the Chief Justice of England, Lord Mansfield, presiding.

Thus the acts of Captain Parker's company of Lexington farmers came before the highest court of England for judgment. The question involved was this: Had they inaugurated a state of war in America which justified their being treated as enemies of the king, or were they peaceable, law-abiding citizens, acting within the legal rights of Englishmen? This would determine whether the killing of our men was done in legitimate warfare or whether it was a barbarous, unprovoked murder, as John Horne had asserted.

Let us look at the character of the men engaged in this trial. Chief Justice Mansfield stands among the ablest and the most learned jurists in English history. Such is the judgment of Campbell in his "Lives of the Chancellors," and such was the judgment of Daniel Webster, although it is told that on one occasion, when an advocate named Dunning was pleading before him, Mansfield interrupted him and said, "If that is law, I will go home and burn my law books." "My lord," said the advocate, "you had better go home and read them."

Undoubtedly, Mansfield stands as one of the highest authorities in English jurisprudence, but he was the stoutest and rankest of Tories. He maintained that the Americans should be brought to their knees before their petitions were considered or their requests listened to. He had drawn the odious Stamp Act and opposed its repeal. Such was the man before whom the case was to be tried. Lord Thurlow, the attorney-general and afterwards Lord High Chancellor, was, of course, an able and earnest partisan of the king. He brought the action in his own name, and conducted the trial with the determination to secure a conviction and the severest and most ignominious punishment. We have no means of knowing the jury, but they were, undoubtedly, carefully selected for the purpose. Such were the conditions under which John Horne was brought to trial with the intention, on the part of the government, to disgrace and crush him.

It is interesting to consider, for a moment, the kind of man the government had undertaken to punish. He was a graduate of Cambridge University, a minister of religion, a gentleman, and a scholar. He had been the ardent friend of our cause from the beginning of the controversy, opposed to the Stamp Act, the Boston Port Bill, and every other measure for oppressing and coercing our people. He was a vigorous debater, keen and quick in sarcasm, pitiless in vituperation and ridicule, and fearless in the advocacy of liberal opinions. This may be fairly inferred from the account he himself wrote of the trial and from the fact that he has been suspected to be the author of that remarkable series of letters over the signature of Junius. It was a puzzle that confounded the sharpest intellects of that day and has never been satisfactorily solved. The government put forth all its power and wit to find out who was Junius, but it sought and probed in vain. Week after week and month after month the ministers were writhing under the merciless attacks of Junius, but were helpless as babes under the lash of his invective and ridicule. Who he was is a secret sealed up in some unknown grave, but certain it is that John Horne had the wit and wisdom to have written those able, bitter, and irritating letters which inflamed the ministers with impotent rage. Horne was a master in the knowledge and use of English, and old Dr. Johnson, of dictionary fame, said he should adopt some of John Horne's etymologies if he were to write his dictionary again. This man is best known in history as John Horne Tooke. Having fallen heir to a fortune of $40,000 left him by a Mr. Tooke of Purley, he adopted his name.

When John Horne was brought to trial, he had the most able, skilful, and brilliant legal talent of England arrayed against him, and yet he conducted his own defence. It would probably have made no difference in the verdict, even if Edmund Burke had defended him. His conviction was a foregone conclusion. Here were the circular letter and the receipt given by the bankers for the £100 transmitted to Dr. Franklin for the Lexington sufferers. Here were the witnesses who heard his speech in the public meeting. It was impossible to deny these things. Indeed, he boldly acknowledged them, and on them the attorney-general rested his case. Horne brought on, as a witness, a Captain Gould, an officer in one of the British companies that fired on Captain Parker's men on Lexington Common. He was wounded and captured in the afternoon and held a prisoner at Medford, where he said he was most kindly treated until exchanged. His account of what occurred on the Common does not differ, materially, from that of many others. He could not tell which side fired first. He said, "We fired and rushed on, huzzaing."

Horne sought to show that no war existed, that no provocation had been given, no opposition to the march had been made, and hence the firing was a deliberate, unprovoked murder, justifying him in his charge, since he had stated only the simple truth. But Captain Gould testified that, as soon as they crossed the river into Cambridge on the night of the 18th of April, he heard firing of guns and cannon, to alarm the people. This, I believe, was a mistake. I have found no such statement before. I have always supposed that the first alarm, save that given by Paul Revere to the people along the road, was rung out from the old belfry on the Common. However that may have been, the judge ruled that the firing of alarm guns and cannon indicated, virtually, that a state of war already existed, that fighting had begun, and hence it was a slander and a crime to speak of the action of the king's troops at Lexington as murder. Horne

made a plea of four hours in his own defence, the case was
given to the jury, and a verdict of guilty promptly returned. Subsequently, when sentence was to be passed,
Horne petitioned for a suspension of judgment on the
ground that no indictment had been found against him,
the action having been brought by the attorney-general
without this previous legal step being taken. Here,
again, the judge decided against him, saying that the
attorney-general had a right to bring the action on his
own knowledge and without a previous indictment by
the grand jury. Lord Thurlow then moved for judgment against the prisoner, and proceeded to state what
it should be. He said there were three different pen-
alties which might be inflicted for this offence. First
by fine, which, he contended, would be far too lenient,
involving little hardship or disgrace, and, therefore, totally inadequate for the punishment of such guilt. The
second was by imprisonment, which was open to the same
objection. It did not impose a punishment such as Horne
deserved, and he had boasted that the jail did not alarm
him, since he could employ his time pleasantly and profit-
ably in study and writing. He urged that Horne should
be subjected to a punishment which would render him
forever infamous in the sight of men. He said: "He has
insulted our Lord the King, maligned his ministers and
defamed his army by asserting that the men killed at
Lexington were murdered. He ought to suffer the most
humiliating and repulsive penalty that the law allows
for such an offence. My Lord, I move that John Horne
be put in the pillory and exposed to the scoffs and jeers
of the people."

But the judge was more merciful than the attorney-
general, and only sentenced the prisoner to a fine of £1,000
and imprisonment for one year and until the fine was
paid; and this sentence was executed upon him. The

fine and costs amounted to $6,000, a sum equal to twice
that amount in the money of to-day. It was duly paid
and the term of one year passed in prison. But this was
not all it cost John Horne to be the friend of America and
the advocate of liberal political opinions. He was followed almost to his dying day by persecution in one form
or another. Giving up his church in Kent, being unable
to minister to it while in jail, all doors were closed and
barred against him when his term in jail was ended. He
studied law, but was denied admission to the bar on the
ground that he was a clergyman, and, therefore, could not
be a lawyer. Then, receiving the splendid bequest of
Tooke, he adopted his name and devoted himself to political life, running twice, unsuccessfully, for Parliament.
On the third attempt he was elected, but here, again, misfortune attended him. He was refused admission to the
House on the ground of being a clergyman, and so his
political ambition came to an ignominious end. It would
seem that the government dogged his steps, determined
to harass and crush him for his obnoxious sentiments.
Of an impulsive and generous nature, Horne, like thousands of English liberals, was deeply interested in the
French Revolution. It was confidently believed that
the dawn of universal liberty had broken upon the world,
and that free governments would be everywhere established. It was a glorious hope, appealing to all generous
hearts, but doomed to quick and bitter disappointment.
Horne was charged with conspiring for the overthrow of
the monarchy in England. He was arrested and brought
to trial on this accusation. Strange to say, Lord Thurlow, who had secured his conviction in the former case,
was employed to defend him, which he did successfully,
and Horne was acquitted. We hear no more of his political offences in advocating the principles of the American
and French Revolutions. He was free to pursue his

favorite studies and enjoy the fortune left him by his admiring friend, in whose honor he called his great work on etymology "The Diversions of Purley."

In 1812 the earthly career of this strong, earnest, enthusiastic soul was closed. A faithful friend to our cause, he suffered obloquy and loss for maintaining that that little band of patriots on Lexington Common were standing there for the rights of all Englishmen and that those who fell were brutally murdered, martyrs in a holy cause. Surely, his name, his deed, his spirit, should be recalled and honored in the place whose name he made familiar to all England by the zeal and heroism he showed in our defence.

Lord Brougham says of the severe sentence imposed on Horne, "Thus a bold and just denunciation of the attack made upon our American brethren, which nowadays would rank among the very mildest and tamest effusions of the periodical press, condemned him to prison for one year and fine and costs amounting to £1200." But this punishment was light compared with those which had been inflicted upon some of the English Puritans a century and a half earlier, when men were whipped, fined, and imprisoned for not using the English Prayer Book in worship. Slow, indeed, has been the growth of liberal principles in Church and State. The freedom and tolerance which we possess as a birthright and enjoy, almost unconscious of the blessing, have come to us through the suffering and sacrifice of thousands now unhonored and forgotten. It becomes us to perpetuate the names and deeds of those that are known, and hold them up for inspiration to noble patriotism and worthy living.

THE ANTI-MASONIC MOVEMENT, PARTICU-
LARLY IN LEXINGTON.

By Albert W. Bryant. Read February 11, 1902.

Those whose tenure of life enables them to attain to the age of an octogenarian will then, if their experience coincides with mine, be aware that their mental and physical powers are waning.

When those faculties become impaired by age, there is a desire to recall to mind scenes and reminiscences connected with the earlier portion of our lives, in preference to the current topics of the present time.

Any event that serves as a reminder of some occurrence long since past is received with pleasure, especially if the recalled event be one that happened at that period of our life when, as young persons, we entered the arena of action with hopes and aspirations, alert to secure health, wealth, and happiness.

As these recollections pass before our mental vision, they bring forth pleasant memories, and it seems as if we were living over again some of our earlier times.

Recently I chanced to see a notice that appeared in a New York newspaper, over the name of an individual who announced that, being dissatisfied with what he had witnessed and heard in receiving the first degree in a Masonic Lodge, and the refusal to refund the amount he had paid, he was preparing for publication an exposition of his experience. This notice brought vividly before my mind some scenes and events that occurred in Lexington, as well as elsewhere, in connection with the Anti-Masonic Crusade between the years of 1830 and 1840,—that political episode which reached its climax during the campaign which elected Andrew Jackson in 1832 President of the United States. It commenced a few years previous, and continued a few years after that election.

I have voted at seventeen Presidential elections since that time. If all the political controversies and partisan feelings of those campaigns could be united, they would not equal what was manifested in the campaign of 1832. I was deeply interested in the effort made to exterminate Freemasonry, for the reason that my father and most of my male relatives were members of the fraternity.

I heard the accusations that the Masonic institution was guilty of perpetrating every crime named in the calendar of crimes, from fraud to murder.

Such open and undisguised statements furnished a cause for more than ordinary interest. Also the time was near at hand when I should be privileged to cast my first vote, which was another incentive to ascertain the truthfulness of those wholesale accusations.

Therefore, I do not recall to mind any occurrence I ever witnessed that is impressed more vividly upon my mind than that crusade, and yet I feel a reluctance in attempting to comply with several requests from members of the fraternity to furnish an account of that exciting period.

Seventy years have passed since that warfare, and it cannot be expected that memory will be sufficiently retentive to give more than a meagre account.

I have recently examined the reports of several committees appointed at an Anti-Masonic Convention held in Boston. I will defer reference to the reports of the committees, while I collect a few thoughts about Freemasonry and the obstacles it encountered in the eighteenth century; then consider the causes that led to the noted crusade in 1830, the methods that were pursued, and its final collapse.

The Masonic institution has now and ever has had within

its domain those maintaining their own individual opinions upon every shade of religious and political matters;
those following the various pursuits in life, from the
peasant to the king upon the throne; also those whose
opinions upon the economics of the times are as divergent
and unlike as daylight is from darkness. Notwithstanding the wide range of opinion maintained by its members,
one of the most exacting of lodge-room requirements is that
private opinions, however much cherished, shall for the
time being be set aside, so that, in entering the lodge, all
may be one in thought and purpose, thus assuring harmony, which is the strength of every institution. It also
shows that the members meet and part upon the plane of
equality. Another observance strictly enforced is that
no political or religious subjects, or anything not connected with the interest of the fraternity, are permitted to
be discussed.

It would most assuredly be anomalous if, with the wide
and varied range of thought which I have referred to as
existing among the members of the institution, there
were not some who would become lukewarm and indifferent; also dissenters as well as seceders.

In one of the Anti-Masonic reports it is stated that in 1732
a public movement was made to suppress the progress
of Freemasonry. If this statement is correct, it must have
been to create a public sentiment against the institution
of a lodge which probably was being considered at that
time, because the first lodge was not instituted until a
year later.

The plea of doubtful expediency was set in motion and
that the concealment of its doings made it a dangerous
menace against the security of our government.

The movement suddenly collapsed by reason, it was
said, of the assassination of the instigator. Freemasonry
was introduced into the country July 30, 1733, when a

lodge was instituted by Henry Price, the first Provincial Grand Master of New England, who received a warrant from London, dated April 13, 1733, with authority to establish a lodge in Boston, which became the first regular lodge on this continent, and was called St. John's Lodge. In 1749 a charter was granted for another lodge, which made the second one in this State.

These lodges continued their mission without opposition except now and then a few words from some one who probably considered he was performing a meritorious work.

In 1762 an effort was made to arouse public sentiment, and the oft-repeated cause of alarm was given, but the apathy of the people frustrated the attempt. It was reported that the leader of the scheme met the same fate which his predecessor did in 1732. In 1783 the two lodges that were instituted in 1733 and 1749 were given permission to unite, by reason of having lost by fire their charters and records, and retain the name of St. John's Lodge.

During the last decade in the eighteenth century Freemasonry was unusually prosperous. Lodges were formed in Lexington, Concord, Dorchester, and other places. This activity influenced two individuals, whose intellectual abilities consisted mainly, as it appears, in their own imagination, to come before the public reiterating what had been stated before, but they soon retired without gaining much notice.

I come now to the time when I can remember much that I heard and witnessed, and will endeavor to recall to mind some of the causes that led to the Crusade against Freemasonry and the attempt to form a new political party.

The contestants for the office of President of the United States for the term from 1824 to 1828 were John Quincy Adams and Andrew Jackson The parties were so evenly balanced that there was no choice by the people, and the

House of Representatives at Washington gave the election to Adams.

The disappointment gave to the Jackson party a determination to succeed, if Jackson should become the nominee for another term, and this intention was kept alive through criticisms and denunciations during the Adams administration.

In 1827 Adams and Jackson were again candidates for the office of President. It was a vigorous campaign, and many assurances made: if Jackson should be elected, the administration would be conducted on a basis of justice and equality, partisan influence unnoticed, office-holders undisturbed, and public demands speedily and amicably adjusted.

The contest was close, but Jackson was elected by a small margin. Jackson was known as a devoted Mason, and had been Master of a lodge in Tennessee for nine years. Immediately after his inauguration in 1828 he selected the members for his cabinet.

As soon as it was known that every one of them was a Master Mason, it was at once construed as his intention to connect Freemasonry as far as possible with his administration. While the campaign was in progress which elected Jackson, a report of a sensational character was circulated. The report stated that William Morgan, a resident of Batavia, a town in New York, had suddenly disappeared, and it was rumored that he was abducted and probably murdered for exposing the secrets of Freemasonry, of which order he was a member.

The report of the New York affair, together with Jackson's cabinet appointments (although he subsequently disclaimed having any other motive than competency, it being simply a coincidence that all were Masons), awakened an earnest and decided opposition to the Masonic fraternity. The advisability of taking immediate measures towards its suppression was publicly discussed.

There was, however, such a variety of opinion expressed that no definite plan of action could be harmoniously adopted. Therefore, the conservative portion recommended a delay until the proceedings in the Morgan case were developed by the evidence given in court.

I will here recall a few events that were enacted during Jackson's first term. The course he pursued tended to promote more discord and distrust in the political ranks than ever before. Instead of carrying out the promised assurances made during the campaign, the old maxim, that "the spoils belong to the victors," was soon adopted.

In an address delivered at Worcester, October 14, 1832, Daniel Webster, at that time a member of the United States Senate, said, "The Constitution declares that every public officer in the State or General Government shall take an oath to support the Constitution of the United States," but the President in a veto message used the following language: "Each public officer who takes an oath to support the Constitution swears that he will support it as he understands it, and not as it is understood by others."

If this interpretation was carried out, it would raise every man's private opinions into a standard for his conduct, and the foundation for all law and government would be destroyed.

The veto power was originally understood as a power vested in the President as a guard to be used when exigencies in hasty or inconsiderate legislation might occur. It was used twice by Washington, once by Madison, and once by Monroe. The frequency of its use by Jackson brought forth many protests. He also adopted the silent veto, which is a veto without giving a reason or an explanation.

His attack upon the United States Bank, denying its constitutionality, came when it had been in existence for thirty-five years, and had been approved by several Presidents and Congress, during that time. He removed nearly two thousand office-holders during his first term as President, in contradiction to statements made in his campaign. These several extracts relative to his administration will, I trust, give an idea of his wilfulness and perversity.

The course that was being pursued by the administration was hailed with pleasure by the Anti-Masons, as it was furnishing material for their cause. While Jackson's first term of office was passing, the Anti-Masons were active in considering plans toward uniting the different factions. Before any plan had been adopted, the frequency of reports of the cases that were on trial in the courts in New York, resulting from the Morgan episode, increased the excitement to such intensity that about two hundred persons held a meeting in Boston in August, 1829, and assumed the responsibility of making a preliminary movement for the purpose of allaying the excitement; also to ascertain what response it would elicit.

After the meeting had organized by the election of a chairman and secretary, a committee of eleven persons were elected, and called "The Suffolk Anti-Mason Committee," of which none were Masons.

The committee were instructed to "investigate the nature, principles, and tendency of Freemasonry," and report at some future meeting.

As no provision had been made for calling a future meeting, this committee issued a notice for a meeting on December 30, 1829, for the purpose of electing a State Committee and such other business as might be deemed expedient.

One hundred and forty-five members were present. After the meeting was properly organized, the Suffolk Anti-Masonic Committee was elected as the State Anti-

Masonic Committee, with authority to call conventions and have the general control of all demands. This meeting was the first formal act towards establishing the Anti-Masonic political party. The meeting continued in session until January 1, 1830.

In furtherance of plans for providing for future demands several committees were appointed, and the duties that would be required were apportioned, such as the public press, finance, lectures, and correspondence.

At the April and May elections for 1830 Anti-Masonry appeared at the polls in some towns, as the legislature at that time convened in June instead of January, as now. Representatives and senators were chosen at those meetings. In the Senate for that year there were three Anti-Masons out of forty members, and twenty or twenty-five in the House of Representatives out of four hundred and fifty members. The number of members were so few that no action of note was attempted.

Only a few brief extracts can be made from the committee's reports, as they were not only lengthy, but each committee prefaced their report with a full account of all the iniquities that were ascribed to the Masonic fraternity.

On June 1, 1830, a committee that was chosen January 1, 1830, to report a set of resolutions that were adopted in a convention held at Faneuil Hall, were directed to lay them before the Grand Fraternities of Freemasons in Massachusetts, setting forth the wickedness of Masonry, and requesting the honest Masons to disfellowship the Grand Lodge of New York. This document was sent as directed, but was returned without note or comment. Other similar communications were addressed to three of the Grand Masters and other prominent Masons, from whom no response was received.

The committee was further instructed to report what measures it is proper to recommend to the people to guard the equal rights of our citizens and the faithful administration of justice. The committee reported the following resolutions:—

1st, That the people, in giving their suffrages at the polls, should express their disapprobation of the Masonic institution.

2d, That the membership of the Masonic fraternity should be made, by statute, a sufficient ground for challenging a juror, when one party is a Mason and the other is not.

3d, That the patronage of the people be extended to such persons who give to the public the facts connected with the principal operations and tendencies of Freemasonry.

4th, That extra-judicial oaths be made by statute penal.

On June 1, 1830, a committee, consisting of eleven persons who were elected January 1, 1830, and instructed to prepare resolutions to be presented to the Grand Encampment of Massachusetts, issued a set of resolves which were publicly addressed as instructed. As the resolves are quite lengthy, a synopsis only will be given:—

1st, That all societies should be open and amenable to the public.

2d, That the disclosures of Freemasonry that have been made show the system to be selfish, revengeful, and impious.

3d, There is evidence that Masons, impelled by some of their obligations, have robbed their country of the services of a free citizen.

4th, That the system is one and indivisible, whether consisting of three or fifty degrees, and answers for its conduct wherever situated.

5th, That, in view of the premises, we respectfully request the Grand Fraternities of Freemasons in this State to disfellowship the Grand Lodge, Grand Chapter, and Grand Encampment of New York.

6th, That the Anti-Masonic State Committee be directed

to furnish each one of the Grand Officers of the several Masonic departments in this State with a copy of these resolutions.

7th, That, in our opinion, the oaths imposed by Freemasons are profane, and entirely destitute of any moral obligation.

After these resolutions had been published, a denial of the truthfulness of the entire allegations appeared, signed by twelve hundred Masons in and around Boston.

Upon the return of the resolves without acknowledgment, the committee requested that one or more of the allegations be selected, and the committee would make oath of their validity: then the Masonic Fraternity could have suitable ground for commencing a suit at law.

The request was unnoticed, but at the next session of the Grand Lodge the Master in his address said, "If our institution is ever abolished, it must be done by ourselves: none else are able to do it, and certainly none else are competent to decide whether it should be abolished or not; and I would advise those in the Crusade against us that we can manage our own affairs without volunteer aid."

In proof that there was no intention of relinquishing the institution, at a meeting of the Grand Lodge in June, soon after the resolves were published, a vote was passed to erect a building in Boston for their accommodation, at a cost of forty thousand dollars ($40,000). The cornerstone was laid October 14, 1830.

A committee was appointed to inquire whether intelligent Christians or churches can fellowship with Freemasons without bringing reproach and disgrace upon themselves and the Church. As their report is not only lengthy, but repeats much that has been previously stated, only the two questions asked by the committee and their answers will be noticed. "What is a Church?" is the first one to receive attention. " It is," the committee answers, "a holy society, incorporated by the God of heaven, sustained by his power and grace, from the beginning of the world to the present time, and destined to flourish forever in the world of glory. It is the kingdom of heaven upon earth; the temple of the living God, or habitation of the Spirit, and the school of Christ, in which immortal souls, by spiritual culture, are trained up and prepared for their heavenly inheritance. The Church is the pillar and ground of the truth; the salt of the earth; the light of the world, and of Jehovah. The fulness of Him filleth all in all."

On the other hand, "What is Masonry?" To this question the committee replies: "It is an earthly institution; self-created by a company of brick-layers and stone-cutters, formed in London, June 24, 1717; upheld by terror, propagated by deception, guarded by a sword; stained with blood, shrouded in darkness, covered with crimes; filled with blasphemies, and threatening with destruction all who renounce their allegiance to the mystery of abominations. Masonry in its whole length and breadth is as Anti-Christian as it is Anti-Republican. Its tendency is to corrupt, and ultimately to undermine and destroy, all our civil and religious institutions, and spread infidelity, despotism, and misery through the earth. Such being the nature and spirit of the two institutions, no fellowship can exist between them; and the clergyman having in charge a church within which these two elements exist is not only practising duplicity, but is also disgracing the character of the church, and ought not to remain in fellowship with the profession."

The committee having charge of the financial department complained of a lack of funds. They gave their time, paid their own expenses, but were asked to settle other demands. The disposition to talk and offer advice was more frequent than that of contributing to the funds, but not so agreeable to the committee.

The committee having charge of printing and correspondence reported that the publishers of newspapers were evidently acting in league, and, to avoid discussion or public controversy, refused to publish any of the proceedings of the Anti-Masonic party.

To overcome this difficulty, five or six new papers were started. Their success was not very promising. The lack of patronage kept them in a languishing condition, and so financially embarrassed that their standard for general information was so deficient that their duration was uncertain.

The committee to provide public speakers and assign them to places where their services would be most effective reported that many complaints were received from speakers that they were not respectfully treated in some places,— a disposition to make disturbance or ridicule seemed to be the chief desire.

The most plausible reason for these complaints was because the speakers were seceders, or Anti-Masons. If the speaker was the latter, he was told, "You know nothing about Masonry except what some renegade has told you."

If the speaker was a seceder from Masonry, he would be termed a turn-coat, and more or less distrust and doubt as to his honesty made his services unimportant.

The committee who had kept in touch with the court proceedings in the Morgan case made a detailed account. A brief abstract from the report will show that the final result is not surprising, when a small portion of the contradictory testimony given in court is seen. There were trials for murder, trials for complicity, also trials as accessory before the act.

There was sworn evidence that Morgan's body was weighted and sunk in the water above Niagara Falls, also that men were seen watching below the Falls for his body;

there was evidence that he was afterwards seen in Canada; furthermore, there was testimony that he sailed from Westerly, R.I., for New Orleans, and was then in business in Mexico.

There was evidence given that the whole matter was a political scheme, to be used as a measure toward the formation of a new political party.

When the cases were on trial in the courts, there were criminations and recriminations; and the proceedings resembled a judicial burlesque rather than a court of justice. To sum up, the whole gigantic episode after several years in litigation ended without accomplishing any intelligent or satisfactory result.

I will here heed the admonitions of my thoughts, which are that I ought to be rebuked for continuing this political harangue so far as to be tedious, and I will only refer to the final appeal of the Anti-Masonic State Committee to the public, and especially to the Masonic fraternity.

The committee entertained hopes that the Whig party would put in nomination a man who was not a Mason; then the Antis would join with them, and this would unite the several factions then existing among the Antis; and strengthen the Whig party sufficiently to secure the election of their nominee. This act on their part might secure some recognition that would be of benefit to them in the future.

The nomination of Henry Clay, who was an ardent Mason, banished all their hopes in that direction. The committee were aware there was no prospect of electing William Wirt, their candidate.

After deliberation it was concluded that the only course consistent with their views was to sustain the nomination of William Wirt of Maryland for President and Amos Ellmaker of Pennsylvania for Vice-President, made at a national Anti-Masonic Convention held at Baltimore, September 30, 1831.

It seems that the committee thought it might not be entirely fruitless to offer a suggestion and make an appeal to the Masonic fraternity.

The committee addressed the fraternity as gentlemen of intelligence, and kindly requested them to review the facts that had been disclosed, and sustained beyond doubt, of the evil and pernicious tendencies which are a dangerous menace to the country.

The following suggestion was offered: that, if the Fraternity would withdraw from the institution, surrender the charters of their lodges, and dissolve the Grand Lodge, the act would allay party strife, restore harmony, bring peace and friendship. By thus doing, a magnificent ovation would be theirs to receive, with a season of public rejoicing.

The assurance was given that such a praiseworthy act would not pass unrewarded: the public offices would be at their disposal without contestants from their present opponents.

"If your conclusions are adverse to this proposition, we wish you to consider the forebodings that are surely ominous."

"The information which the Anti-Masonic movement has furnished the public in regard to your institution has laid a foundation that will erelong remove every vestige of Masonry. If your choice is to adhere to its perpetuation, then an ignominious defeat and disgrace awaits you in the near future."

This generous appeal and offer from the committee will bear comparison with the prayer of the negro who, when on a ship that was in danger of foundering in a gale, commenced to pray to the Lord, promising to give Him a lump of gold as big as his head. The captain asked him why he made such an offer when he had no gold. He replied only, "Yes, tell 'em so till I get ashore." The committee could only say the same.

The Anti-Masonic political party was organized December 30, 1829, and its existence as a party terminated at the close of the Presidential campaign in the month of November, 1831. It had at its inception all the knowledge, information, and material for carrying out its purpose and intention. The question is very naturally asked, What caused so short a duration?

In the first place it was founded upon one idea, and only one,—the extermination of the Masonic institution. It had not a single associated issue, such as finance, tariff reform, and other subjects that make up the platform for a campaign, though it did have a horde of office-seekers.

The excitement from Jackson's cabinet appointments and the Morgan affair soon subsided. Jackson explained that his motive in selecting his cabinet was solely ability. In the Morgan case, after a lengthy period in litigation, all that was gleaned was a confused mass of contradictory testimony that would not establish the charge.

The managers of the organization were not only inefficient in executive ability, but were handicapped in various ways. Financial aid was wanting; the public press silent for their cause; the public speakers received with distrust; and public sentiment indifferent.

They found the Masonic fraternity intrenched within their fortification, with wealth and the press at their command. They saw members of the order connected with the various departments of public service. With no allurement or device could Masons be enticed to engage in any general discussion.

This state of things continued until the election in 1831; but, when it was known that William Wirt received only seven electoral votes, while thirteen States were represented at the general Anti-Masonic Convention, the party subsided at once.

For several years after this election those who had been

active workers for their cause felt their defeat so keenly that they sought every opportunity to create dissension in municipal affairs.

It would be difficult to realize the intensity of party strife during the campaign alluded to. Common civility, neighborly intercourse, and personal recognition were to a great extent ignored. An instance was known where a man forbade his brother, who was a Mason, to enter his house (this in Lexington).

Party interest became so infectious that the ladies were occasionally heard. I remember of hearing a neighbor of mine relate a discussion which he overheard between his wife and another lady. One was advocating the election of Henry Clay, the other of General Jackson, and the latter got a little the better of her opponent. The one praising Clay inquired somewhat sharply, "Who is Jackson, anyway?" The other said, "I vum, I don't know, but my husband says he is a mighty smart man, has been a great fighter, lives somewhere down South, and, if he is chosen President, he will make things whiz."

Notices were publicly posted in this town in 1831, stating that Professor Allyn of Worcester would give an entertainment at the Academy Building on an evening named, when an account of the purposes and the success of the Anti-Masonic party would be given, and the opening and closing of a Masonic lodge correctly illustrated; also the conferring of the three degrees in Masonry would be given.

This announcement awakened an earnest desire in me to witness this performance for reasons before stated. The professor appeared with a retinue of assistants sufficient to officer a lodge, with the exception of a chaplain. The introductory part of the entertainment was an address by the professor, giving his experience and explaining his reasons for denouncing Freemasonry, and also his withdrawal from any connection with it. He professed to be conversant with every part or phase of the institution.

He appeared to be well educated, an easy speaker, and quite eloquent. His manner of illustration was such that he gained the attention and won the sympathy of the audience. He stated,—after familiarizing himself with every department of Masonry and seeing how inimical and dangerous the oaths and obligations were to a republican form of government, as the oaths were considered paramount to and superseding all others, whether of a civil, social, or religious nature,—that courts of justice were obstructed, inasmuch as the oaths compelled a member to screen and protect a brother Mason in any condition, right or wrong. As no honest person, who had the welfare and respect of the community at heart, could subscribe to and maintain such pernicious requirements, he was convinced that it was his duty publicly to make known the dangerous tendencies that were being promulgated under the garb of charitableness. Therefore, he flattered himself that the course he was pursuing would commend itself to all loyal citizens. Furthermore, the success already obtained by the exposition of what would surely happen from Masonry, unless speedily checked, had enlightened the minds of the community; and he was assured that the death knell of Masonry had been sounded, and its doom sealed. Vigilance, however, would be required to stop any sudden attempt towards its revival.

When the preliminary remarks were concluded, his associates were placed in their respective positions as officers of a lodge, and their duties explained; the lodge was declared open in due form; the conferring the three degrees followed, with an explanation of the grips, obligations, and such other formalities as he stated were necessary to the correct manner of giving them.

While the exercises were passing, occasional stops were

made for the purpose of calling the attention of the audience to the manner in which plots or plans could be concocted by the secrecy enjoined.

The audience filled the large room completely, with the exception of the space used for the lodge exercises. The enthusiasm was great, and the applause was nearly continuous. The room was well adapted for the purpose, it being fifty or sixty feet in length, with seats rising from the centre towards the sides of the building, and extending lengthwise of the room. In the centre a clear space twelve or fifteen feet in width gave ample room for all that was needed for their purpose.

My attention was so completely absorbed with seeing and hearing, with a memory sufficiently retentive, that, after the proceedings were closed, I could repeat nearly verbatim all the obligations, passwords, and the duties of the several officers, as performed by each one.

The day after the lecture I met an individual who was free-born and of good repute, whose character was above reproach, whose word was unquestionable, who had not a known enemy, and was an aged member of Hiram Lodge. I told him what I heard and witnessed the previous evening, and repeated the several obligations and the way they were given. I also stated that the professor and his associates were strangers; it was a question with me whether their representation of Masonry was truthful or false.

I asked him if it was really true that he had himself ever subscribed to the like. His reply was, "Did the lecturer say they were true, and that he pledged his word and honor that he would conceal, never reveal, but keep sacred and gave a token of his sincerity?" "Yes, he did." "What reason did he offer for his unfaithfulness?" "Because, if they continued to exist, these were measures that endangered the peaceful relations of every form of society, and could be used to subvert the ends of justice, by the power held and controlled by sworn secrecy; and he could not conscientiously hold sentiments that were traitorous to the laws and welfare of his country."

"How did he propose or expect his views to be carried out?" "By the ballot box."

"Now, if I were to admit I had taken such obligations, and should, after promising by my honor (that which is the foundation of every person's character) that I would conceal, never reveal, what had been intrusted to me by an act of friendship, then, under the pretence that something wrong might happen, sacrifice my word upon my honor, by throwing all my self-respect into the unreliableness of a political party,—if I were to do this, would you or any one have more respect for me? would my word or promise be more reliable? what would your estimation of me be as a citizen? would not all that I may possess that is worth having be lost? in short, would you have the least respect or confidence in me?" "No, I should not." "What you heard last evening came from the lips of a self-confessed perjurer, which I consider a source beneath notice."

A relative of mine who resided in Boston, a merchant, president of a bank, also prominent in military affairs, was approached by a committee from the Anti-Masonic State Committee, soliciting funds for the campaign; also his co-operation with their party, stating his influence would be beneficial to them, and he could be rewarded by receiving the nomination for any office within their gift.

His reply was: "I am neither a Mason, nor an Anti-Mason, but a conservative, or what you term a 'Jack.' Before, however, I should comply with your request, I must be informed of the purposes of the party, and the reasons for such a party." They replied that Masons at heart were traitors to our government; also, under the shield of secrecy, were enabled to plan and carry out any nefarious design they chose; the only means to prevent their purposes was their extermination through the ballot box.

In answer to their statement my relative replied: "My wife has five sisters whose husbands are Masons, and three brothers who are also. Her father is a Master Mason, and a charter member of a lodge.

"I am of course intimately acquainted and connected with them in various capacities. I know them to be business men, upright in their dealings, with credit that will command any reasonable amount. They also hold positions of trust and respect. Look with me in another direction, if you please. You assert that Masons are traitors. Was Paul Revere, when taking that hasty midnight ride on the 18th of April, 1775, to Lexington? Was that the act of a traitor? When Warren and Putnam stood on June 17, 1775, on Bunker Hill, were they guilty of treason? When Washington immortalized and made sacred that elm-tree in Cambridge by standing under its branches with uncovered head and uplifted hand, swearing allegiance, and taking command of the American army, did he prove himself a hypocrite?

"If I have been correctly informed, every officer of note in the Revolutionary army was a Mason, with but one exception: that was Benedict Arnold. No, gentlemen, if I were to accede to your request, I must forfeit the respect and friendship of a large circle of friends and relatives. I shall not ignore and cast aside my firm convictions that your assertions are not supported by facts. My belief is that you are following a misguided opinion. The result will be a complete defeat."

Some of the leaders of the Anti-Masonic party for several years after its collapse watched every opportunity to revive recollections of the past. The following were some of their attempts, which are a fair representation of their folly.

After I became a member of the fraternity, a man who had been one of the leaders in the campaign came to see me for the purpose of giving friendly advice (in his opinion) of the unwise course I was pursuing by connection with any secret society. When he finished his harangue, I asked him if the right to enjoy his own opinion was a privilege that belonged exclusively to himself. "Yes, and I swear I will maintain it." "Are you not willing that others may have the same right?" "No, unless they think as I do."

At a meeting of the selectmen of Lexington at which I was present, as town clerk, held for the purpose of revising the list of jurors, one of the board, who was an Anti-Mason, moved that the names of all Masons upon the list that had not been drawn be stricken off, and the name of any man who was a Mason, not placed on the list as revised.

The chairman replied: "I am not a Mason, but probably know about the order as much as you, which is nothing. I do know that the characters of the Masons in this town are above reproach or suspicion, and for us to approve of the motion would cast aspersion upon their integrity, and also show a disregard for the oath of office which we have taken as selectmen."

The murder of Dr. Parkman was committed by Professor Webster in a building in Boston used for medical purposes. Webster was arrested, and, when arraigned for trial, an individual, who had been and was still opposed to Masonry, said to me: "Now you will not only have a verification, but also see the truthfulness of the fact that the oaths taken by a Mason compel him to screen or protect a brother Mason, however strong or conclusive the evidence may be against him.

"'The trial of Webster is only a farce, as Webster is a Mason, and five of the jurors on the panel are also, and they will never dare convict him. Now mark my words, and see if they do not prove true."

After the trial was ended and the verdict rendered, I informed him that his predictions had not been verified, and I wished to ascertain when those five recreant jurors, who had violated their oaths (according to his statement), would receive their reward. His reply was more expressive than elegant: "Damn it, they dared not do otherwise, as the evidence was so conclusive against him as not to admit of a doubt, and public opinion was so strong of his guilt that a different verdict would have been an outrage. They therefore concluded that the excitement was so intense that the violation of their obligation in this case would be condoned."

The persistency in continuing to speak against secret societies seems inexplicable, when it is clearly seen that all the attacks hitherto have proved to be of an advantage to such societies instead of otherwise. They have served to awaken an interest which has caused investigation and has increased the number of societies to such an extent that there is scarcely a hamlet in the country but has a secret society of some kind. Some little time since a convocation of clergymen was held in Boston. The question as to the cause of so many vacant pews in the churches was discussed. The trend of the opinions was that secret societies, especially Freemasonry, were the principal reason.

No longer ago than last December, at a meeting held at a church in Boston, the same subject received a large share of attention. One minister said that secret societies should be denounced from the pulpit, and that no one belonging to any secret society should be a member of any church.

A brief space of time given to analyze the significance of "secrecy" would suffice to convince any candid or thoughtful mind of the importance and necessity for its use. That it is an important factor with the business portion of the community is fully demonstrated by observation. The manufacturer, merchant, mechanic, artist, capitalist, professor,—every man, whatever his calling, must make use of secrecy.

In taking this retrospective look, it is seen that Freemasonry cannot claim to be coexistent with the settlement of this country, and the church is the only institution that can; but in the first quarter of the eighteenth century Freemasonry can claim to be contemporaneous in existence with the government and church institutions in America.

For one hundred and seventy-five years these institutions have pursued their respective missions. There is a remarkable similarity or coincidence in their experiences.

The government institution has had its foes from without and within. It has resisted foreign aggression, and defeated insurrections, at the cost of millions of dollars and hundreds of thousands of lives sacrificed for its defence. It has had traitors, embezzlers, and knaves of the darkest hue. Three of its chief executive officers have fallen by the hand of the assassin. Notwithstanding it has encountered aggressiveness of every description, it has prospered and progressed, so that its present position commands respect wherever civilization exists.

The welfare of the church has occasionally been disturbed by foes without and foes within; its sacred robes have been used to shield crime; apostates have gained entrance into its domain; some of the leaders have fallen in dishonor. It has continued its course onward, receiving merited respect; and to-day is recognized as a beacon-light and guide for life.

The institution of Freemasonry, as it nears the close of the second century of its existence in this country, has also had foes from without and from within; traitors and disturbers have attempted to subvert its purpose and check its progress; all obstacles have proved incentives for renewed action; increasing numerically; extending in area, so that at present its strength and influence are such that no array against it need be expected.

If the names of those who have been adversaries of these three institutions were gathered, in what estimation or respect would their memories be held?

One word would be the answer,—"Derision."

THE EXISTENCE AND THE EXTINCTION OF SLAVERY IN MASSACHUSETTS.

By Rev. C. A. Staples. Read April 8, 1902.

In the early history of the Plymouth Colony, founded in 1620, there is no mention of negro servants or slaves. The Pilgrims were an humble, poverty-stricken folk, and probably few among them could have owned slaves, had they so desired. Among the passengers in the "Mayflower," however, some are spoken of as servants in the more prominent families, like Dr. Fuller's, Governor Carver's, and Governor Bradford's. They were probably young men bound to them for a term of years by contract and in consideration of being transported to this new and unexplored land. Some of these so-called servants became freemen and founded families from which have descended noted citizens of our country. But, as population and wealth increased, negro slavery gradually crept in. Bristol and Newport on the southern boundary of Plymouth Colony were engaged in the slave-trade, annually importing from Africa cargoes of negroes to supply the home market in New England. The difficulty of procuring permanent household servants and laborers led to the bringing of these importations from the Guinea Coast by the wealthier families and holding them as slaves. It came to be regarded as a mark of social distinction in the community. The families owning two or three negro servants were considered of superior importance, occupying the highest position of respectability and influence. Thus the holding of slaves became not uncommon in the Old Colony where, at first, there was social equality and where the democratic spirit largely prevailed. A hundred and twenty-five years after the landing of the Pilgrims slaves were found in almost every town of the colony, but the whole number only amounted to one hundred and thirty-three in the census of 1754.

The Massachusetts Colony was composed of a different class of people. In Winthrop's party were men of considerable wealth, allied to the English nobility and graduates of Cambridge and Oxford. It is said that Massachusetts has never contained so large a percentage of college graduates as in the first half-century of its history. Certain it is, also, that some of the emigrants brought with them fortunes of from ten to forty thousand dollars, equal to more than twice that amount in the money value of to-day. This was the case with Winthrop, Dudley, Endicott, Saltonstall, and others. Thus, from the beginning, the Massachusetts Colony had a fair degree of wealth, learning, and refinement, and it has given character to our subsequent history. Many families among the settlers were accustomed to trained household servants, and, not able to procure them here or retain those brought from England, they were the more inclined to buy and hold negroes as slaves. Against a strong popular sentiment in opposition to slavery and especially to the slave-trade, wealthy families bought men and women for service in the household, the shop, the store, and on the farm. Slaves came to be numerous in the large towns, especially along the seacoast and in the eastern portion of the Massachusetts Colony. In the census of slaves for 1754 the whole number in the province, then including both Plymouth and Massachusetts Colonies, is 2,566, of which Suffolk County held 1,300, or more than half the whole number; Middlesex, 361, of which Lexington had 24, and Lincoln 23. In all Worcester County there were but

88.   Essex County had 435, and Barnstable but 83, indicating that the slaves were confined chiefly to the larger towns, where there was most commerce and most wealth.   The number of slaves continued to increase until about the time of the Revolution, and I have seen one estimate of their number at 4,500.

It is impossible to ascertain just when slaves were first introduced into Massachusetts, but it was probably at an early day in its history.   Winthrop took possession of Boston in 1630, having bought out Blackstone, who moved to Rhode Island.   Samuel Maverick at that time had settled on Noddle's Island, now East Boston, and held a few negro slaves.   This is the first mention we have of slavery in Massachusetts.   So far as we know, none of Winthrop's party owned slaves, but, evidently, they were soon brought in by traders from the West Indies, a few at a time, and sold to the settlers.   In "The Body of Liberties," a sort of constitution by which the colonists were to be governed, adopted in 1641, the ninety-first article reads as follows, viz.: "There shall never be any bond Slaverie, villinage, Captivitie among us, unless it be of lawful captives taken in just wars and such strangers as willingly sell themselves or are sold to us."*   It is difficult to understand how any statement could open the door wider to slave-trading and slave-holding than this. "Captives taken in just wars, strangers willingly selling themselves or sold to us," all these may be bought and

---

* This article, omitting the word "strangers," was retained in each revision of the colonial laws.   See a review, by Judge Horace Gray, of legislation in Massachusetts concerning liberty and freedom, found in 14 Allen, at pages 562–563.   One should note that in the declaration from which Mr. Staples quotes, immediately following the quoted language, is this sentence, viz.: "And these shall have all the liberties and Christian usages which the law of God, established in Israel concerning such purposes, doth morally require." If a master was guilty of "cruel or unreasonable castigation," he was liable to punishment as for a breach of the peace; and Judge Gray says that a slave could sue his master for "wounding or immoderately beating" him.   It is worthy of observation that slaves were not debarred from giving evidence in court, even in the trial of white persons for capital crimes.   They were also permitted to testify in suits of other slaves for freedom.—R. P. C.

sold, without scruple, but none besides! What more or better than this could negro stealers and traders ask for the prosperity of their business? Three years before this, viz., in 1638, a cargo of negroes arrived in Boston Harbor and were sold into slavery. Notwithstanding the generous provision of "The Body of Liberties" for their introduction, the number of slaves increased very slowly in the colony, if the statement of Governor Bradstreet, in 1680, is to be taken as correct. In answer to twenty-seven questions asked of him by the British Board of Trade, regarding the government and condition of the colony, he says of the importation of slaves, "No company of blacks or slaves has been brought here since the beginning, except one small vessel from Madagascar with 40 or 50, mostly women and children, which were sold for £10, £15 or £20 each. But they cost the merchants importing them near £40 each. Now and then two or three are brought from Barbadoes and sold for £20. There are, in the Colony, 120 and as many Scots taken in the recent wars with Scotland and half as many Irish." Thus, fifty years after the beginning of the settlement, the number of slaves had only reached 120. From this time on the increase was much more rapid.

Of course, the condition of the slaves in the colony depended, largely, on the character of the families in which they were held. In some cases they were kindly treated, well clothed, fed, and housed, seldom parted from their children or the husband from the wife, and continued for generations in the same family. They were often taught to read and write, learned trades, and became efficient and skilful as carpenters, masons, and blacksmiths, and sometimes bought their own freedom by extra work. On the whole, they were treated well, and, as household servants, were on terms of something like intimacy with the members of the family, though anything like social equality was denied them. They were baptized in the church and admitted into its fellowship and communion, but they had seats assigned them in the galleries of the church, apart from the rest of the congregation.

There were undoubted cases of cruel and brutal masters. There are instances on record where the old and the sick were cast off to die in some cold and dreary outbuilding, or left to starve or freeze, friendless and alone, in the wretched garret of a house where they had faithfully served for many years. Such cases must ever be a blot upon the history of Massachusetts. But the same brutality was shown here, seventy-five years ago, in the treatment of the insane poor. Miss Dix relates such stories of "man's inhumanity to man" here in New England, and they inspired her to do her blessed work of establishing the insane asylum.

The slave-owners were among the most intelligent and religious people of the colony, among whom were many ministers, especially in the larger cities and towns. In 1728 Lexington voted to give Rev. John Hancock £85 with which to purchase a servant. After Mr. Hancock's death in 1752 this slave remained with Mrs. Hancock, I think, until her death in 1760. There is no mention of a negro servant in connection with Mr. Hancock's successor, Rev. Jonas Clarke. He had imbibed too fully the spirit of universal liberty, and would have gladly knocked the shackles off from all limbs and bade the enslaved everywhere go free.

In 1738 the great merchant Peter Faneuil, whom Thomas Hancock called "the Toppingest man in Boston," directs Captain Buckley, then in his employ, to take a load of salt fish on a voyage to the West Indies, sell it there on his account, and invest the proceeds in "a straight negro lad 12 or 15 years old, of a tractable disposition and who has had the small pox." Governor John Hancock was the owner of slaves, and among them was a majestic negro man, Pompey, who acted as his butler. On one occasion, when the governor was holding a banquet at his mansion on Beacon Street, Pompey, in gorgeous livery, was deputed to wait upon the table. The earlier courses had been removed when Pompey went to bring in the tea. The governor was proud of his wealth and the rich and beautiful furnishings of his house and his table, but his special pride and delight lay in his "chinny," which had been collected and brought home by his sea captains trading with the East. These collections were of great extent and priceless value, exquisite in form and color, but fragile as gossamer. Pompey appeared at the door, bearing an immense salver with its precious burden of china, superb in his conscious importance in displaying his master's treasures. He had hardly entered the dining-room when he stumbled and fell headlong upon the floor, making a tremendous crash and shattering the delicate vessels into a thousand pieces. "Pompey," said the governor, "I don't care for my chinny, but I won't have such a confounded noise."

Not infrequently a daughter received a negro servant as part of her marriage portion, and, in their wills, people assigned their slaves to one or another of their children. Francis Bowman, of this town, called on our records "The Worshipful Mr. Bowman," so disposes of his four slaves by will, specifying to whom each one should go. In settling estates it was often the case that the slaves were sold at auction, with horses and cattle, and families were separated, never to be reunited.

Many of the negroes in this vicinity had been stolen from Africa and sold from the slave-ships of Bristol and Newport. Among these was Prince Estabrook of this town, who was, probably, a slave in the Estabrook family. The tradition was that he had been stolen from his home and brought to this country. He was the son of a prince, and hence the name given him here. Like many other slaves, he enlisted in the Revolutionary army and fought for the independence of a people who had robbed him of every right dear to the human heart. He gained his freedom by his service, married here, and remained in Lexington until his removal to Ashby, where he died and is buried. Children and young people were fond of him as a participant in their sports. A young girl in Lexington, when dying, said, "I wish I could be buried in Ashby beside dear old Prince Estabrook." In the history of Deerfield is an account of a remarkable African slave woman in the Wells family in that town. Her name was Lucy. She remembered the awful scene when, a young girl of eight or nine years, she had been seized at her play by the man-stealers and hurried on board the slave-ship. In May, 1756, she was married to Abijah Prince of Deerfield, a respectable negro who had been freed by his master and who, in some way, obtained the freedom of his wife. She was known as "Luce Bijah," and had a reputation for literary talent, was a writer of verses of some merit, and effective and eloquent in speech. They were an ambitious couple, and by dint of hard work and good management they acquired a considerable property. Moving to a newly settled town in Vermont, they became possessed of large tracts of land for the benefit of their children. Their oldest son, Cæsar, served in the army of the Revolution, and, becoming disabled in advancing life, received a pension from a grateful people of $2.66 a month! But, in a long controversy over land titles, Abijah and his wife became involved in expensive litigation. In this Luce Bijah, the former slave woman, led the contest for their rights. She fought the case from court to court, until at last it came before the Supreme Court of the United States. Her lawyers had prepared the case in legal form, but she was allowed to make the final plea, and won her cause. The Judge, Hon. Samuel Chase of Maryland, declared that she made a better argument than he had heard from any lawyer of the Vermont bar. But the poor woman failed in another suit before a tribunal not so open to a plea for justice. Her highest ambition was to have one of her sons receive a college education. To gain admission for him to Williams College, she pleaded with the trustees in vain. For three hours, with indignant eloquence, she pressed her claim, using law and gospel in its support, but to no purpose. They rejected him solely on account of his race. It illustrates how deep-rooted was the prejudice against the negro, in New England, a hundred years ago, and may help us to understand the strength of this prejudice in the people of the South to-day.

It is remarkable that there is no positive legal action of our colonial legislators establishing slavery, nor of State legislators abolishing it. It existed here rather by sufferance and the tolerance of public opinion than by any legal enactment. It was extinguished by no positive enactment, but simply by a decision of the Supreme Court, under the declaration in the State Constitution of 1780, that "all men are born free and equal."

The first protest against negro slavery of which we have any account was made by that grand man, Judge Samuel Sewall, chief justice of the colony, in 1700. In an address entitled "Joseph Gold" he condemns, on scriptural and humanitarian grounds, the buying and selling of our brethren, the children of God, stolen from Africa or captured in war. This is the same man who a few years before, as one of the judges, had condemned to death nineteen men and women accused of witchcraft at Salem. Of this he repented, in bitterness of soul, to his dying day, carrying to the grave a load of self-reproach and remorse. A kind-hearted, conscientious, deeply religious man, misled by that miserable delusion. But he pleaded for that justice and mercy to the slaves which he had denied to the poor victims of the witchcraft superstition.

In 1769 a slave had sued his master for services rendered on the ground that, though born of slave parents, he was yet a free man. "The Body of Liberties" of 1641 defined those who might be held as slaves, but did not include the children of such slaves, and, consequently, they were free. The court sustained the contention, and gave the man his suit and his freedom. This decision was sustained by Lord Mansfield, chief justice of England. No disability of parents, under English law, could descend to their children, and what was true of his Majesty's subjects in England applied to all his dominions.

Twice the General Court attempted to prohibit the importation and sale of slaves in the province, but the action was each time negatived by the Royal governor under instructions from the home government as an interference with English trade. The second time was in 1774, when the controversies that brought on the Revolution had attained great warmth and bitterness.*

The sentiments proclaimed as the foundation of the patriot cause, recognizing the inalienable right of man to life, liberty, and the pursuit of happiness, seemed grossly inconsistent with the existence of negro slavery; and yet some of the most ardent advocates of American liberty were owners of slaves. This inconsistency was obvious to the humblest mind. The opposition became more and more strenuous and determined. The readiness with which the blacks came forward to enlist in the Revolutionary army won for them sympathy and admiration. Some of the towns, in their reply to the Boston Committee of Corre-

* In September, 1776, the General Court forbade the sale of two negroes who had been taken as prizes of war on the high seas and brought to port. Any negroes that might thereafter be so captured the statute also declared should be treated the same as ordinary prisoners.—R. P. C.

spondence, calling upon them to unite in support of the common cause, protested, in the strongest language, against the inconsistency of fighting for their own liberty while holding a race of fellow-beings in bondage, and they asked that measures be adopted immediately to put an end to this injustice and cruelty, that they might deserve the blessing of God upon their cause.

No action was taken in this direction until near the close of the Revolutionary War. In 1780 the State Constitution was framed and adopted. It contained a Declaration of Rights in almost the exact words of the Declaration of Independence. "All men are born free and equal." It is believed that John Adams caused this to be inserted in the document. Whether he did it with the idea of freeing the slaves or not is not known, but the whole thing was accomplished under that declaration, and upwards of four thousand slaves obtained their freedom. It is a strange and interesting story. In 1754 a slave family, Mingo, Dinah, and their infant boy Quork, was bought by William Caldwell of Barre from Zackariah Stone for £108. When Caldwell died, nine years afterwards, the boy was assigned to the widow in the division of the estate. She promised him his freedom when he should reach the age of twenty-one, but, before that time came, she married Dr. Nathaniel Jennison of that town, and died in three years. Quork became the property of the husband, who had no intention of redeeming the promise of his wife. So the poor fellow continued working for Jennison as a slave until he was twenty-nine years of age, when he left his master and went to live with the Caldwell brothers as a hired man on their farm. Here Jennison attacked him when ploughing in the field, threw him down, beat him with the handle of a whip, and with the aid of another man dragged him home, and put him in close confinement. But Quork soon managed to escape, and with the aid of the Caldwells brought an action against Dr. Jennison for assault and imprisonment. This was in May, 1781, and the case came on for trial in the Court of Common Pleas at Worcester the following September. Jennison was convicted, and sentenced to a fine of £50. Thereupon he brought an action against the Caldwells for enticing away and harboring his slave Quork. This action was carried up to the Supreme Court for final decision at the April term at Worcester in 1783, and was tried before the full bench, Judge William Cushing being chief justice. Here the case was fully argued, and the decision rendered that Quork was no longer the slave of Dr. Jennison, but a free man under the Declaration of Rights in the Constitution of the State, and henceforth slavery could not exist in Massachusetts where all men were born free and equal.*

It is a curious fact that, while our court applied this declaration to all slaves, without limitation, the Supreme Court of New Hampshire, where the same language is used in the State Constitution, applied it only to those born after the adoption of their Constitution. Hence slavery existed there until the last slave born before that time died, a period of seventy or eighty years after it became extinct in Massachusetts. The decision rendered by Chief Justice Cushing, striking the shackles from thousands of slaves, is brief and simple in language, but dignified and noble. I quote the concluding sentences. He says:—

* In view of this decision it is not easy to account for the fact, as appears from the case of *Watson* v. *Cambridge*, officially reported in vol. 15, Mass. Reports, page 286, that a slave named Venus was sold at public auction in Cambridge, Mass., in 1793 by the administrator of Samuel Whittemore. She seems to have had some inkling of her rights, for the record says, "The said Venus was present at the said auction, and refused to go into the family of one of the bidders"; and in consequence the auction was suspended for a while. After the sale William Watson, the successful bidder, gave to the administrator a bond in the sum of £200, conditioned to provide suitable raiment and diet for Venus during her life, and at death to see her decently buried. It may be conjectured that this arrangement resulted in part from her own demands and in part from humanitarian sentiments in the family on whose behalf the administrator made the sale.—R. P. C.

"As to the doctrine of slavery and the right of Christians to hold Africans in perpetual servitude and to sell and treat them as we do our horses and cattle, that, it is true, has been hitherto countenanced by the Province laws, but nowhere is it expressly enacted or established. It has been a usage, a usage which took its origin from the practice of some European nations and the regulations of the British Government respecting these Colonies, for the benefit of trade and wealth. But, whatever sentiments have formerly prevailed in this particular, or slid in upon us by the example of others, a different idea has taken place with the people of America, more favorable to the natural rights of mankind and that natural, innate love of Liberty with which Heaven, without regard to color, complexion, or shape of noses, or features, has inspired all the human race. And, upon this ground, our Constitution of Government, by which the people of this Commonwealth have solemnly bound themselves, sets out with declaring that all men are born free and equal, and that every subject is entitled to Liberty and to have it guarded by the laws, as well as life and property, and, in short, is totally repugnant to the idea of being born slaves. This being the case, I think the idea of slavery is inconsistent with our conduct and Constitution, and there can be no such thing as perpetual servitude of a rational creature unless his liberty is forfeited by criminal conduct or given up by personal consent or contract."

This decision, in which all the judges concurred, gave the death-blow to slavery in Massachusetts. It was never called in question by an appeal to the Supreme Court of the United States, but universally accepted as sound law and justice. The negroes generally continued in the service of their former owners, with compensation agreed upon, or remained with them for food, clothes, and care until death. Many, no doubt, were cast off in old age,

to depend upon private or public charity, and much suffering often resulted; but human slavery, with the cruel
injustice and wrong which it involved, was at an end in
the old Commonwealth, swept away forever, not by force
of arms, but by the mightier force of Christian sentiment and principle embodied in that grand Declaration
of Human Rights, "All men are born free and equal,"
opening a path for all to rise to higher life and larger
happiness.

DIARY AND LETTERS OF CAIRA ROBBINS,
1794–1881.

BY MISS ELLEN A. STONE. READ FEBRUARY 12, 1907.

On Sunday, April 27, 1794, there was born to Stephen Robbins and Abigail Winship, his wife, at their home in the East Village, a daughter. This homestead is still standing on Massachusetts Avenue, next below the Brick Store in East Lexington, and in 1920 will be two hundred years old. The father, Stephen Robbins, was fifth in line of descent from Richard Robbins, who was in Charlestown in 1638, settled afterward in Cambridge, and whose descendants were later living at Cambridge Farms, or Lexington. He was a man of strong and dominant personality, with peculiarities which went even to the verge of eccentricity: a kind father, a successful trader, and founder of the fur industry in East Lexington in 1783, which was later carried on by his son and others, and did so much to develop that part of the town. His wife, Abigail Winship, was a direct descendant of Lieutenant Edward Winship, of Cambridge (1635), first of the name in the Massachusetts Bay Colony, also of Samuel Winship, high sheriff of Middlesex County under the Crown, in the days of King George the Second, and was a devoted and affectionate wife and mother, an industrious, pious, and consistent Christian woman.

This daughter was their seventh and last child, and in the little Scriptural flock of Stephen, Samuel, Abigail, Eli, Martin, and Lot, took her place with a name wholly strange and foreign. C-A-I-R-A was the name,—the refrain of one of the wild revolutionary songs that were stirring up France in the Reign of Terror in 1793 and 1794; but it

caught and held the father's fancy, and Ça Ira became
the English Caira,—a name now endeared by association
to members of the family.

As youngest child and only daughter at home, in a
family in very comfortable circumstances, she enjoyed
many advantages of education and opportunity beyond
the average.   Note this item:—

LEXINGTON, September 26, 1804.

Mr. STEPHEN ROBBINS, Dr.,
to Timothy Wellington.

For the tuition of Caira Robbins, 5 weeks, at 25c. per week . .$1.25

Received payment,

TIMOTHY WELLINGTON.

This Timothy Wellington was the son of Timothy
Wellington and Hannah Abbott of Lexington, H. C. 1805,
and later the well-known physician of West Cambridge.

Another item under date of June 9, 1805, though not
immediately connected with Caira, is nevertheless of much
interest, as showing the educational advantages enjoyed
by her sister, and presumably advantages of a similar
character were enjoyed later by herself.   This is Mrs.
Susanna Rowson's bill for the tuition of Mr. Stephen
Robbins's daughter, Miss Nabby.   This gifted author, born
in Southampton, England, 1762, in her earlier years had
been an actress of fair ability, who, shortly after her arrival
in America in 1793, had turned her attention to literary
pursuits with such success that among her works her
novel, "Charlotte Temple," has become almost a classic
in American literature.   Her select school, "for the education of female youth" near Boston, was one of the best
known of its day, and combined with sound intellectual
training instruction in the social usages and polite accom-
plishments of the time.   This bill is as follows:—

NEWTON, June 9, 1805.

Mr. STEPHEN ROBBINS to S. ROWSON, Dr.

To one quarter's board for his daughter Miss Nabby . . . $30.00
" tuition: embroidery and painting 9.00
" paper, pencils & embroidery thread 56
" carriage to meeting 1.00
" ticket and carriage to the play. 2.25
" a large piece of embroidery 10.00
" use of embroidery frame 25
                                                       ———
                                                       $53.06

Received payment

SUSANNA ROWSON.

A copy of Mrs. Rowson's poems, handsomely bound in calf, was presented to Miss Nabby on leaving school, and it still remains among the books of the house.

Varied school advantages were enjoyed by Caira, for among her papers we find these items:—

July, 1809. Attended Miss Swift's School. Did not improve much.

Later:—

1810. Went to Mrs. Haswell's school about the middle of April. Stayed three months.

A reward of merit still exists, in size 2 inches by $1\frac{1}{4}$, dated 1810, May, as follows:—

Miss Robbins. Neat, amiable and improving.

Still later, in 1813:—

Went to school at Westford one quarter with Mary Ann Swan and Betsy Harrington. Mary Ann was sick, left school, and died in the winter.

Her only sister, ten years her senior, Abigail, or Nabby, as she was familiarly called, had married early and "well," as the New England expression is, and made her home in

Montpelier, Vt., where she was in the enjoyment of much worldly prosperity and many social advantages. Thither, for recreation and diversion, her younger sister went, at intervals, during her life, keeping at such times a formal record of such events as seemed to her of interest or moment. In later life these memorials were very miscellaneous in character,—domestic, social, literary, or practical,—and were incorporated into what might be called a "Commonplace Book." An astonishing number of these papers have been preserved, either in whole or in part and is the source from which these notes are made. Let us turn to her diary, where early appears this entry:—

1809, *June* 26. Nabby R., married to James H. Langdon, Montpelier. Took her departure same day. Accompanied her to Billerica. Rode with Dr. W.

Dr. W. was Dr. Thomas Whitcomb, the physician of Lexington, who next year married the widow of Joseph Chandler, and died early. This item calls to mind one of the customs of the times. The invited guests took chaises and accompanied the newly married pair on their way toward their new home, and, when they had gone as far as was convenient, turned quietly back, without the formality of good-byes, until at the last the wedded pair were left pursuing their way alone. This young girl of fifteen went with Dr. Whitcomb as far as Billerica, which was then considered a day's journey.

This item follows:—

July, 1809. Eli R. married to Hannah Simonds. Rode again with Dr. W.

In 1812, April 25, sister Nabby writes and invites her young sister, then eighteen years of age, to come to Montpelier for a visit, and says:—

The bearer of this note, Mr. Bowles, who keeps a book-store here, is a very likely young man. I presume he will wait upon you very politely and willingly. I should like to have you come very much, if you are well enough to come in the stage . . . James H. sends love and says you must come. N.B. If you should not come, send me word how they make gowns.

The diary goes on to say:—

May, 1812. Sister Nabby sent for me to go and see her. Accordingly, I set out from home the 14th day of June. Took the stage at Billerica in company with Mr. L. and several passengers. Not a female until we came within thirty or forty miles of Montpelier.

The details of this first trip may possibly be of interest. They are still preserved, written in a neat, copper-plate hand, with much exactness and precision.

Lexington, June 14*th*, 1812. Set out on a journey for Montpelier, Vermont. Arrived at Billerica the same day. Took supper and lodging that night; breakfast the next morning.

15*th*. Passed through the towns of Chelmsford, Tyngsboro, Dunstable and Amherst, where we took dinner. From thence to Mt. Vernon, Francistown, Hillsboro and Washington. Took supper and lodging.

16*th*. Lemster, Claremont; took breakfast. Cornish, Windsor, Hartland; dined. Woodstock, Royalton; at Randolph supped and lodged.

17*th*. Brookfield, Berlin, Montpelier. A four days journey.

Apparently, the summer passed very pleasantly.

July 4*th*. Attended a ball, very much gratified.

The card of invitation shows that the ball began at 5 P.M. on Thursday, at the Academy, Montpelier.

Aug. 19. Went to Middlebury to Commencement with Mr. and Mrs. L. I rode over with Mr. Pixley, Preceptor of the Academy, who was going to be married, & returned in a carriage with Mr. Mattocks and family.

Mr. and Mrs. L. went to Connecticut. I was sick with the measles.

From Lexington, September 19, 1812, comes this letter from "Your Pa," as follows:—

Little Daughter:

I received yours of September, but no day of the month. You wish to know whether you may stay until spring. Miss Page was here last week with the same request, I understand directed by you. I told her if I knew that Nabby actually wanted you to stay and you desired the same, I should consent, although I should be much pleased to have you come home. Firstly: We should be glad to see you. Secondly: We want your work. You know, yourself, that what you could earn this fall would amount to quite a large amount when you are eighty. You will take into consideration all these things and do as you think best. I have no doubt you will be well cared for. [Then follow items of family interest.] N.B. If you want any of your clothes you must send by teamster. Daniel says he loves you. From your Pa.

Another letter, dated Lexington, February 13, 1813:—

Little Caira:

I received yours of the first, this day. Was pleased to hear that, although you had got the measles, you were fast getting well. I hope you are now entirely well. You say you have not heard from us for a long time. It looks a little like homesick. If that is the case, get Mr. Langdon to help you home and I will pay all expenses. We shall be glad to see you. We have not forgot you, and I hope you will be able to say: "Your father's house has large supplies and bounteous are his hands," etc. Your mother sends love and Aunt Frances sends her love and says she wants to see you. Lot and Daniel send what love they have.

From Your Pa, STEPHEN ROBBINS.

N.B.   By desire of Aunt Francis, I inform you that she has been to Lot's dancing school and stayed most all night. Was much pleased.

These two letters were written on foolscap, sealed with red wafers, and sent by the post, at a cost of seventeen cents each.

June, 1813.   I came home with Mr. L. in a chaise. Stopped at Brother Samuel's in Windsor.

On her return home, after a very pleasant year in Vermont, she went, in August, to Westford Academy, to which reference has already been made. This was a well-known and very excellent school, where she was instructed in reading, writing, orthography, English grammar, plain work, and marking, together with arithmetic, composition, geography, the use of the globe, drawing maps, and muslin work. Letter-writing seems to have been a favorite occupation with young ladies at school, and the fashion of 1813 and 1814 was to carry on a correspondence under a *nom-de-plume*, and quite a correspondence still exists between Evelena Hamilton and Clarinda Fenelon, the latter being Caira. The following is an excuse for not writing a letter:—

CHARLESTOWN, February, 1813.
12 o'clock at night.

I write a few words, having an opportunity to send directly to you, to let you know where to direct your next communication. If you write soon, it may find me in this town, but I cannot tell for a certainty, for we shift our quarters as fast as a vane that is in the power of the wind. Be not offended, my dear girl, at my long silence. I shall not at this time offer an apology, but, relying on the benevolence of your heart, I trust you will not reproach me too severely until you know the cause. You may expect very shortly to receive a long and a tedious letter from

Your sincere friend,

EVELENA HAMILTON.

CLARINDA FENELON.

To return to the diary:—

1814. Spent most of the summer at Col. Page's. Went to fort twice. Saw Peter Conant. Ate chowder for the first time.

In 1816 another journey to Vermont,—a short trip, leaving Lexington May 30, and arriving home the last of June. This time she went by the way of White River,

and returned by Ascutney Mountain. At Hanover, N.H.,
she seems very much impressed with the town.

It contains a college, academy, chapel and meeting-house, and
many other handsome buildings. They are built on a plain and make
a very handsome appearance.

At Brookfield, Vt., she writes:—

We passed through "The Gulf," a narrow defile between two
mountains towering almost to the skies; the sides of the mountains
almost perpendicular, thickly covered with various kinds of trees.
A narrow stream, rushing with impetuosity over the craggy steep and
broken rocks, added to the wild and romantic appearance of the place.
The unbroken solitude and the lonely situation, with the approach
of evening, inspired a solemn awe.

For a year or two no more long journeys, but much
diversion and amusement at home.

1817, *February* 9. A cold Friday. Mr. Bowman's party.

June 11. Dr. Hamlin called to give me an invitation to go to the
circus. Dr. Spalding, E. M. and L. W. took tea with me.

November. Went to the theatre: "The Mountaineers."

1818, *December.* Attended the Exhibition Ball, on a visit to
Mrs. C.

(Mrs. C. was Mrs. Carter, wife of the well-known writ-
ing-master, Henry Carter, of Boston.)

December 18. Went to the theatre with Mrs. C. Saw "Othello."

December 19. Went to the Juvenile Association in the Latin
School.

December 21. Attended the theatre; saw Wallack in "Richard
Third," and "Love à la Mode."

(This Wallack is presumably the father of Lester Wallack
of our day.)

1819. *February* 10. Attended the theatre with Miss P. Saw
"Innkeeper's Daughter," "The Rival Soldiers" in conclusion.

June 4. Attended the Mechanical Exhibition. But it was not
all gayety.

June 8. Listened to a eulogy on Shubel Bell, Esq., by Knapp, in Mr. Ware's church.

Aug. 19. Celebrated the obsequies of the late Thomas Webb, Esq., at Boylston Hall; the eulogy by Mr. Dean.

Shall I read an invitation to a ball, written with some formality February 10, 1818?

Mr. Barrell presents his compliments to Miss Robbins, and informs her that on Monday evening next there is to be a ball, given at the new hotel in Weston, to which he asks the pleasure of her company, and, as on her acceptance will depend Miss Page's going, he will feel obliged by her sending an answer to this note by to-morrow or next day (in the affirmative) in order that Miss Page may make up her mind. Mr. Barrell is not certain that Miss Page can make it convenient to leave home, or the weather might prevent, in which case Miss Robbins will not feel disappointed. At any rate, should Miss R. accept, and nothing occur to prevent Miss P.'s, he will be at Lexington with her by noon on Monday. Mr. Barrell was not informed until this morning that the ball was to take place so soon. Otherwise, he could have informed Miss Robbins of Miss Page's determination before asking her, and he hopes it will serve as an excuse for his manner of doing it.

Boston, Tuesday morning, 10th February, 1818.

12th of February.

Mr. Morrill was to have taken this note the day on which it is dated. Mr. Barrell, however, is now enabled to say positively that Miss Page depends on her acceptance and is making the necessary preparations usual on such *important* occasions. Mr. Barrell will take it for granted that Miss Robbins does accept, unless it is utterly out of her power, in which case she will please send word on Saturday. Mr. B. cannot hear of any other excuse from Miss R. than indisposition, as he has no doubt of her being compensated for any trouble it may give.

Whether Miss Robbins went to the ball or not, I do not know. Doubtless, however, she did, and enjoyed it.

The diary now extends over several years in great detail, giving items of personal, family, and local interest, but I doubt very much whether they would be of special interest to this gathering.   Occasionally an item stands out.

1820, *December* 1.   Was much interested in reading Thaddeus of Warsaw.   What a noble youth!

Dec. 3.   Attended meeting.   Text: Matt. 20: 22.   A very good sermon by Mr. Coleman.   The end and aim of religion is an acquiescence in the will of God.

Dec. 6.   An explosion of powder at Chelmsford took place yesterday.

Dec. 12.   A pleasant sun, but cold.   A standard was presented to the Ancient & Honorable Artillery Company by Col. Monroe.   Address read by Mr. S. Chandler.   An alarm of fire in the evening.   It proved to be a chimney; blazed out ten or fifteen feet.

While on a visit in Boston, she "attended the Ampitheatre; saw 'The Rival Soldiers,' and went to the Gallery of Fine Arts."

1821.   *Feb.* 12.   Went to the dancing school at West Cambridge.

Feb. 15.   Mrs. Smith and all my cousins W. from Cambridge here.   Took a sleigh ride, drank mulled wine—a pleasant evening.

Feb. 19.   Attended Mr. C.'s exhibition and a ball on Concord Turnpike.

Feb. 22.   Attended the funeral of Mrs. Davis Wellington.

Mar. 8.   Attended a ball in town.

Mar. 18.   Four couples posted.

(which means that four notices of intentions to marry were read.)

1821, *April* 16.   Watched with Mrs. Swan.   Snowed very fast during the night.   Attended funeral of child and assisted in preparing mourning on that occasion.

April 23d.   Attended Mrs. Bray's Benefit in Boston.   Very much gratified.   "Lots of fun."

April 25.   Attended a wedding in the Stone chapel.   Did not like so much ceremony.

April 26. Domestic affairs call my attention.

May 8. Resigned my office of drudge to abler hands.

May 12. Rode to West Cambridge shopping, called on Mrs. Bowman.

May 16. Have heard of a widower that wants a wife.

20. Attended meeting. Walked. Wore my spencer, was cold. Heard Prof. Ware from 2 Tim. 1: 10.

May 29. Made some preparation for Election.

May 30. Election. A great deal of company in the neighborhood.

June 2. Took tea with Mrs. Morrell, Miss Betsy Holbrook and Mrs. Holmes from Natick.

June 3. *Sunday.* Attended meeting. Heard Mr. Briggs for the first time in more than a year. He preached from Psalms 39: 13. An exercise very appropriate to his own condition. C. Reed posted. To-morrow will be Artillery Election.

June 22. Walked to the Appleton Farm—fine prospect of more than 15 towns.

After a round of visits to cousins in the country, she makes a visit in Boston, and August 13, in evening, on the Common saw The Cadets. "The music excells my highest conception, particularly the bugle."

She spends an evening reading "Kenilworth," and notes on the 18th that "The Cadets left this morning at an early hour."

August 25. Funeral of Parnell Monroe, about my age. How frail we are!

August 29. Commencement Day.

Sept. 18. Mr. Estey and Miss Ann Esterbrooks to dine. Report that the Queen died.

Sept. 20. Went to Boston. Balloon. M. Guille ascended.

Nov. 19. Misses Wellington called—not at home, very sorry.

Nov. 20. Finished a gown; made pies.

Nov. 26. Funeral of Mr. Asa Locke.

Dec. 30. *Sunday.* Mr. John Fessenden, a native of this town, preached. Text: Eph. 5: 20. "Giving thanks for all things unto God." A good discourse. He spoke better than I apprehended.

1822. *Jan.* 29. A ball in town.

Jan. 31. Received word to attend a ball at Leachmere's Point.

Speaking of callers on a certain evening in February, she says:—

Disappointed at their coming this evening. Disappointments are connected with all our human calculations, but it requires considerable fortitude to bear the ills of life with composure.

July 4. Commenced the study of French. Heard oration in Faneuil Hall by Mr. Dunlap. Oration in Old South by John G. Gray, Esq. Dined with ——. Took tea with Mrs. Storrs. Fireworks in the evening. Very much pleased.

Aug. 28. *Tuesday.* Attended the Collegiate exercises. Had a very good seat.

Thursday. Went in to the Meeting House. Oration by Mr. ——. Poem by Peabody.

Sept. 18. Company from Boston. Peaches in perfection.

In May, 1823, she took a trip to Belfast in the newly made State of Maine, a two days' sail, returning to Lexington at the end of the month, which trip she thus describes:—

E. came to stay until May when we sailed for Belfast, Maine. Had a pleasant and quick passage of two days. Found all well and very happy to see us. Spent a fortnight very pleasantly.— Fortune teller.—Sailed for Boston the 20th. Anchored at Owl's Head the 21st. Went ashore. Dined at Esq. Adams. Spent a day in rambling about the woods, skipping stones, rolling bowles. Went on the summit of a mountain, called Owl's Head, on which a light-house has since been erected.

22. Called up at 3 o'clock to go on board. Very fair in the A.M.—Whales.—A fog lasted until next morning.

23. Out at sea all day. Anchored near Boston Light at 2 o'clock.

24. In P.M. anchored near Weymouth Bridge.—A Sea dog. Mrs. P. left us in the evening. Put up at Mr. B.'s in Germantown, a singular family.

25. Attended meeting at Quincy. A heavy thunder shower. Walked in the evening.

26. Took Packet for Boston, then a carriage to Mrs. Stone's.
27. Returned to Lexington.

In 1825, in September, she starts on a trip to Connecticut, returning in the middle of October. This is interesting by reason of the route taken. Starting from Lexington, she goes direct to Waltham, Weston, Marlboro, Shrewsbury to West Brookfield, Springfield, Longmeadow; then crosses the Connecticut River at Ware House Ferry in Connecticut, and finally reaches Hartford. Was very much struck with the sight of a blind girl sewing; sees Mr. Gallaudet of Deaf and Dumb Asylum fame. Finds New Haven "a beautiful place, regularly laid out with a handsome square in the center of the city, on which stand the colleges, statehouse, church, etc." At New Haven takes a steam packet for New York, stays but a couple of days, and returns to New Haven again. Notes that

The church yard at New Haven is laid out in parelclograms, ornamented with trees of various kinds, weeping willows, handsome tombstones, with that of Humphreys Pierrepont Edwards. Dr. Percival, the poet, has a house—no windows in sight.

She seems to enjoy her trip, and returns to Boston by a different route; namely, through Coventry, Mansfield, Wilmington, Pomfret, Uxbridge, Milford, Medway, Medfield, Dedham, and Roxbury, and Boston.

But most interesting of all her travels, and the one which made a lasting impression, was a trip in 1828 to New York City, thence up the Hudson, via Lake Champlain, to Montpelier, Vt. This was followed later, in July, by a more extended journey, in company with her sister and husband, West along the newly constructed Erie Canal to Buffalo and Niagara Falls, then into Canada. At Kingston they took boat down the St. Lawrence to Montreal, Quebec, and the falls of Montmorenci, returning overland to Montpelier. This might very properly be called the Grand Tour of those days,—a journey of some 1,476 miles, taken in the space of thirty days, and made by horse, stage, canal, carriage, packet, and steamboat; a trip involving much fatigue and no little determination, but safely and satisfactorily made, and a source of great pleasure to her then and in after-life. Her diary at this time is written in much detail. She seems to have been an intelligent traveller, very appreciative of natural beauty, and to have been keenly observant both of places and persons. It is interesting to note how people travelled to New York in 1828. First to Charlestown, in the hourly; thence to Boston. Then from Boston to Dedham, where one breakfasted at 37½ cents, by stage on to Providence, at a cost of $2.50. At Providence one took the steamboat for New York, price of ticket $6. At New York, a hack, 50 cents. After seeing the sights of New York, the steamboat "Independence," Captain Cook, took one up the river to Albany, price $4. Stage journey to Whitehall on the edge of Vermont. At Whitehall one took the steamboat "Franklin," Captain Wiswell, to Burlington, fare $3; at Burlington, the stage to Montpelier, $2. Many interesting sights are seen on the way, among others, at Burlington, through the politeness of Captain Harrington, Mr. Gould's new house, "a splendid establishment—lamps suspended from the centers of the rooms, beautiful gardens, yellow roses, and peonies in bloom."

In New York, then a city of sixty thousand persons, she walked down Broadway in a white muslin dress with two embroidered ruffles with insertions of lace, and cape to match,—all her own handiwork, wrought and made especially for the occasion. White chip hat, faced with blue and edged with netted lace, completed the costume; and with her small, trim figure, dark hair, blue-gray eyes, and youth, she must have presented a very attractive appearance. The dress and the hat still exist, and were shown me by herself long years after, when telling the story of her visit to New York. A silhouette of her is still in existence, and shows her to have been of a peculiarly pleasing personality, which family and other traditions bear out as well.

Arrived at Vermont, she writes the following letter to her father:—

BERLIN, Thursday, June 12, 1828.

Dear Father:

I left New York on Sunday morning at 7 o'clock in the steamboat "Independence," Capt. Wiswell, and arrived in Albany the same evening. Distance, 150 miles. Left Albany at 5 o'clock next morning in the stage and rode to Ft. Edward and took the Packet-boat "Lafayette," and arrived at Whitehall at nine in the evening. Distance, 75 miles from Albany. Stayed at Whitehall until next day at 2 o'clock in the afternoon. Took the steamboat "Franklin," Capt. Sherman, for Burlington, and arrived there the same evening. Distance, 75 miles. Left Burlington in the stage 5 o'clock next morning and arrived here at 12 o'clock yesterday. I have had a very pleasant journey. The scenery on the North River was beautiful. It exceeded my expectations. They had a very heavy shower above Troy which made a great many breaches in the Canal. We passed the place where the Canal gave away in Stillwater, and washed the mail stage, full of passengers, out of the road. They were all well drenched, but not otherwise injured. The mail was found next day. I had a fine view of Mt. Defiance, Ticonderoga, Mt. Independence, and Crown Point. The stone building, three stories high, is still standing. [This item was of particular interest to her father, because, as a young man, he had served as a soldier at Fort Ticonderoga] . . . Mother will not feel any concern about me now I have arrived safe here. You would not be afraid to go in the "Franklin" that plies on the lake, for it is said it is so constructed that should the boilers burst it is doubtful if a drop of water would come into the boat. All desire love. Your affectionate daughter,

CAIRA.

With Buffalo and its situation she was very much pleased, but at Niagara was greatly impressed with the falls, the most stupendous piece of natural scenery she had ever seen. She seems to have had great facility with her pencil, and a sketch of the falls remains, very true to life, as a basis for a larger effort, to be made later, with colors indicated in the margin. Seventy years afterwards the writer passed through that same valley in company with Miss Susan B. Anthony; and, as we read aloud this diary, Miss Anthony, who knew the country well, was very much struck with the exactness of the descriptions and their general character. Reference made by Miss Robbins to some local incidents of seventy years before corroborated in Miss Anthony's mind events of which she, as a child, had heard her mother speak, and rendered this diary of peculiar interest to her.

Two letters written at the time give a very interesting account of her journey:—

BOSTON, January 27, 1829.

My dear E.—

As there is some prospect of sending a line to you by private conveyance, I shall venture to write. It is a long time since I have heard from you. Why do you not write? Perhaps you mean to retalliate but I assure you I would write oftener if I had an opportunity to send. . . . You requested me to write about my journey. It will give me pleasure. I believe I told you I was not pleased at Saratoga. There were a great many people there when I was there. I saw but very few I was acquainted with, and they all appeared to be in the same predicament, staring at each other to see if they could not, among the crowd, recognize a familiar face. We took the stage from there to Utica. Fortunately, one of the passengers happened to be a merchant from Peterboro, an old acquaintance of mine. I say fortunately, for you well know how convenient it is to have a gallant when one is traveling. He was only going to Utica, but, finding company, he continued with us to Rochester: just one week. I was sorry when he left us. The ride from Saratoga to Utica is very pleasant, being by the side of the Mohawk most of the way. You have heard much of the banks of the Mohawk. Ballston, about nine miles from Saratoga, is much the pleasantest place, in my estimation, but Saratoga is "all the go." Utica is a very pleasant place and large. It contains about 7,000 inhabitants. We stopped there two or three days: Saturday, Sunday and Monday; we took a hack and went to Trenton Falls, about 14 miles, a most romantic and beautiful place. I must see you to give you a correct idea of the falls and scenery around. A young lady from New York was drowned there about a year ago. You may have heard of the circumstance. We returned to Utica at night and took the Canal boat for Syracuse. It was the first time I was in "the Grand Canal," and I have often thought since of the name I heard a Quaker give it, it was so appropriate. He called it a ditch. I am sure it is most like riding in a ditch of anything.

The second is dated Lexington, February, 1829.

My dear E.—

My hasty letter which I wrote you a short time since has, I presume, reached you before now, in which I gave you a sketch of the least interesting part of my journey. If I recollect aright, I was describing our ride from Utica to Syracuse, when I was called away. In continuance, then, I will proceed. At Syracuse we stopped half a day to view the salt works, at that place and Salina, connected with the former place by a lateral canal of $1\frac{1}{2}$ miles in length. Vast quantities of salt are made at these places: some by boiling, and some by solar evaporation. From a cupola, we had a fine view of Onondago Lake, two or three villages, and the salt works, said to cover 300 acres of land. We took the stage from Syracuse early in the morning, passed through several pretty villages, where a few years ago the wild beasts of the forest held undisputed sway. Auburn is a large place. The State Prison is located here. It is a noble building. We crossed Cayuga Lake on a bridge one mile in length, passed Seneca Falls, through Waterloo to Geneva, a beautiful village situated on the n. w. bank of Seneca Creek. There is a college at this place and many pleasant situations with gardens. Fifteen miles from Geneva is Canendagua, the handsomest village, in my estimation, of any on our route. The location for a town is not as beautiful as Buffaloe, neither is there so much business done, but

there is a degree of neatness and elegance which attracts the eye of
the stranger and impresses one with the idea that they are a social,
enlightened, independent and happy people, and I was afterwards
informed by a merchant who served his time there that that was
the case.   I could write you a great deal of this and many other
places, but must be more concise or I shall not have room to write
you of those places you most wish to hear: Rochester and Niagara.
Of the first, I have little to say in favor of it, and of the other I can
give you no just conception; but to proceed methodically.   After
leaving Canandagua we took a circuitous route in order to see the
"Grand Embankment" of Rochester.   There a hewn stone acque-
duct goes over the Geneva River, consisting of eleven arches.   Canal
boats in line in the evening have a beautiful appearance.   The gentleman who had accompanied us from the Springs procured a chaise &
we rode down the river three miles to Greece, called upon Mr. A.
Blodgett, who was much surprised to see me; returning we viewed
the falls which are about 66 ft. high, and are really very interesting.
There appeared to be a great deal of business going on and a great
many to do it: a mixed assembly of people from every direction: a
great many run-aways ("I guess").   I have a right to guess.   There
are about 12,000 inhabitants, 5,000 more than at Utica.   There are
many handsome buildings, streets broad and will be cleared out in
the course of a few years and look more respectable, but it is astonishing to see how much has been accomplished within a few years.
I left my companion here with regret and proceeded on our journey
in the "big ditch" to Lockport.   After traveling 60 or 70 miles
on a perfect level, we here struck the mountain ridge, which is surmounted by five magnificent locks of 12 ft. each, making an ascent
of 60 ft., connected with five more for descending.   They make
a grand appearance on your entrance.   We spent two or three days at
Lockport.   Here the excavation commences, and continues three
miles through a solid rock, from 20 to 30 feet deep.   We continued on
in the canal boat, as being the most easy way of travelling, to Buffaloe,
about 30 miles from Lockport.   As I have observed before, this is a
very beautiful location for a village.   Every house but one was
burned in 1814.   It now contains 6,000 inhabitants.   It is laid out
handsomely with broad streets and bids fair to be eventually the
prettiest village in that section of the country.   We took the stage

from Buffaloe and crossed the river two miles below on Black Rock, into His Majesty's Dominions, and had a very pleasant ride on the bank of the Niagara, 15 miles to the celebrated falls. There was nothing in the appearance of the river that indicated our near approach to this stupendous cataract until within about two miles of it, where the rapids commenced. We heard a rumbling noise about four or five miles above the falls, which *I* should not have noticed had I not been listening. At the hotel, within a few rods, the noise was much less than I had expected. As I felt that it was very uncertain whether I should ever be there again, I was determined to see all that was to be seen if it was possible. Accordingly, I rose next morning long before sunrise, rallied our party, consisting of Mr. and Mrs. L., two gentlemen from the city of New York who had accompanied us from Lockport, and myself, and sallied forth to view one of the greatest exhibitions in the world. Before we had proceeded far, two of our party (Mrs. L. and one gentleman) left us, but the rest of us continued on, and after scrambling over and under and between rocks for two hours, we returned to the hotel with, as you might well suppose, an excellent appetite for an excellent breakfast; after dispatching which, we all again set forth and went onto the Table Rock, descended the stairs and went underneath it. Here it is that one feels, more than at any other place, the sublimity of the scene. I did not venture behind the sheet of water, for I was told there was nothing to be seen but eels, and, besides, I was then as wet as if I had been in a shower, and I did not care to again crawl, for the name of it. Here, again, the same part of our party left us, and we went on a short distance below the falls and crossed over in the ferry boat in safety to the American side, having a panoramic view in passing. We ascended the bank and crossed the bridge that is thrown from the mainland to the Island which divides the river unequally above the falls. This is a beautiful little island; from it and the approach we had several fine views. Lately, some dexterous hand has thrown a foot bridge from the island to the very brink of the falls, where you can look down into the chasm beneath. After taking a view from every point, and refreshing ourselves at a house by the way, kept for the accommodation of visitors, we re-crossed the river and returned to the house between three and four o'clock, with another excellent appetite for dinner. Conceive, if you can, the beauty and sublimity of the scene, for I am unable to describe it. Imagine an immense body of water of the most beautiful green you ever saw, from the great chain of lakes above, tumbling over a precipice of 158 feet; clouds of fog and spray, variegated with the Sun above and the beautiful rainbows beneath; and you may have some idea of it. I was highly gratified, and was willing to leave as our company was going, but had you been there, I would gladly have spent a week to "behold those scenes so wild, so rude, so beautifully sublime." But I am drawing to the end of my paper, and can only say of the rest of my journey, it was pleasant. We went from the Falls to Montreal, a distance of 400 miles; from there to Quebec, 170 miles; returned to Montpelier by St. John's on Lake Champlain. The whole distance from Montpelier and back was 1400 miles; only about 300 of it did we traverse the second time.

Other travel was enjoyed by Miss Robbins at various times later, but in 1847 her father died, leaving her mother very advanced in years. From that time on until her mother's death, five years later, in her 91st year, she was very closely confined at home. The following extract from the mother's will best characterizes these years of devotion and care. After making due mention of her other children, she leaves all her personal estate, whether money, household furniture, or clothing, "to my only remaining daughter Caira, to her absolute disposal, as a partial remuneration for her uniform kindness and attention to me during my declining years."

After her mother's death she still continued to live in the house in which she was born, happy in the companionship of a schoolmate and lifelong friend, and later of a cousin, until her death, in 1881, in her 87th year.

Apart from any special interest that her relatives may have in her life, the community in East Lexington have this. In her will, among other items, occurs this one:—

Should a public reading-room ever be established in East Lexington, I give the sum of Fifty dollars to assist in establishing it, and twenty volumes of my books, to be selected by my Executor.

In 1885, when a reading-room was opened, which has since become the East Lexington Branch of the Cary Library, Miss Robbins's executor placed upon its shelves, among other books,* her own copy of Shakespeare in twelve volumes, being the Monroe & Francis first American edition.

From a mass of quotations found among her papers, poetical, philosophical, and religious, but which may all, perhaps, be classed under the title "Elegant Extracts," I close with these from the poet Thomson:—

> Well-ordered home, man's best delight to make;
> And by submissive wisdom, modest skill,
> To raise the virtue, animate the bliss,
> And sweeten all the toils of human life,
> This be the female dignity and praise.

and

> An elegant sufficiency, content,
> Retirement, rural quiet, friendship, books,
> Ease and alternate labor, useful life,
> Progressive virtue, and approving Heaven.

---

* Miss Robbins had a private collection of several hundred volumes of standard literature, —a circumstance quite unusual in any Lexington home during her time. Following is a list of some of the works that were donated agreeably to the provisions of her will:—
"Captain Cook's Three Voyages to the Pacific Ocean," 2 vols.; "Historical Sketch of the Great Revolution," by Samuel G. Howe, M.D., 1 vol.; "Numa Pompilius, second roi de Rome," par Florian, 1 vol.; "Paradise Lost," 1 vol.; "Poetical Works of Thomas Campbell," 1 vol.; "The Vicar of Wakefield," by Dr. Goldsmith, 1 vol.; "Life of Dr. Benjamin Franklin," 1 vol.; "Authentic Account of an Embassy from the King of Great Britain to the Emperor of China," 1 vol.; "Views of Society and Manners in America," by an Englishwoman, 1 vol.; "On the Formation of Christian Character," by Henry Ware, Jr., 1 vol.; "The Green Mountain Boys," an historical tale, 2 vols.

THE REV. JONAS CLARKE, MINISTER AND PATRIOT.

By Rev. Charles F. Carter. A Sermon preached at Lexington, Sunday, July 28, 1907.

Walk about Zion, and go round about her: tell the towers thereof. Mark ye well her bulwarks, consider her palaces; that ye may tell it to the generation following.—Psalm xlviii. 12 and 13.

With commendable judgment the Committee on Old Home Week has devoted this first Sunday to the commemoration of the founders of the city, and I have simply extended their idea by making it apply to one of the founders of the Commonwealth. Many considerations make this fitting. It is always wholesome to measure the cost of any good thing that comes into our life, that we may gain a keen appreciation of it, especially when we ourselves have not been called upon to pay that cost. Knowledge of what has been expended, not only of money, but of nerve, of thought, sometimes even of life-blood, is fitting, to arouse in us the sense of appreciation that otherwise might become dulled. We are so apt to take many of the great blessings of life as part of our natural right and customary privilege.

Considering the most valuable things, the things are few for which we pay the cost. We are beneficiaries all, not only dependent primarily upon God himself as the giver of all good, but in very large degree dependent upon our fellow-men who have lived before us and wrought in our behalf and secured blessings into which we have entered. We cannot ever pay such a debt as this to those who have provided these benefits for us. The point of honor is to do our best to hand on to those who follow an equivalent for what we have received.

This indebtedness to the past has often been noted in respect to education. We need not dwell upon it. It is not so often mentioned in respect to the civil advantages that accrue by reason of government and those standards of social order that become essential to security. These things are so well established that, ordinarily, we no more think of examining them than we do of looking at the foundations of our house every time we enter it. Yet there these foundations are, and any defect in them would be a calamity. It is well to appreciate what it cost the men who laid them there.

There were blocks of granite principle that had to be hewed out by laborious thought. They had to be shaped and fashioned and placed in public view, so that other men could see their value, could come to feel that they were sound and reliable. Then they had to be drawn from this quarry of thought by the strength of public opinion and to be placed where a national life and a new social order could rest upon them, and there men had to fight and die, that these foundation stones of the Republic might be anchored in their enduring place. It cost something to raise the towers of state, even to the laying of the foundations on which they rest; and we need to tell it to the generation following, that they become not unmindful of the great price wherewith our liberties were secured.

Alas, when our people (and I fear there are many such to-day) forget the labors of the fathers, and accept life simply as opportunity for individual pleasure, losing the sense of responsible membership in the great body politic! It is a disgrace to receive benefit from your fellow-men who have lived in other generations and not to try to do your part in handing on some benefit to those who shall follow you,—as great a disgrace as it is for a man to buy goods and then never pay for them. We need the recall that such a day as this provides.

A concrete instance is furnished in this town of historic
association that gives us one very definite unit of the val-
ues that constitute our heritage. It is not my purpose
to enter extensively into the details of the life of Jonas
Clarke. They are known to you in outline. Many of
them are of very great interest, and more are still available than have yet been made public. Rather would I
direct special attention to the public service he rendered
in the formation and establishment of our national life.
Three scenes are typical, as they disclose the minister-
patriot in characteristic address.

The members of the Ancient and Honorable Artillery
Company, impressive in their uniforms and dignified in
their bearing, as the men of that time were, have assembled
in the meeting-house in Boston. They have asked a man
from one of the farming towns (Cambridge Farms it once
was called) to come in and preach to them; and the
invitation itself is an indication of the repute in which this
man was held. He enters the pulpit, carefully attired,
his great sack-wig adding to the impressiveness of his
bearing, though to us it might be the occasion of a smile.
But the man has native dignity and force, and his commanding presence finds a suitable organ in his penetrating and
powerful voice.

What kind of discourse are these men to hear? They
are not men playing soldier and decorating the occasion
with the elegance of their uniforms. They have been
called upon for service before, and they know that serious
business may be theirs at any time, although it would not
be justifiable to imply that they were anticipating revolution. This was in 1768, and peace pervaded the land.

But what did this parson do? He takes this theme:
"The Importance of Military Skill, Measures for Defence,
and a Martial Spirit in a Time of Peace." It seems to have
a familiar sound. Some object to the sentiment to-day,

yet I fancy they would not object to it when placed in the
setting of this early day when aggression was to be feared.
With insight he chose the period in Judah's history when
Jehoshaphat succeeded to the throne. His text was this:
"Next him was Amasiah the son of Zichri, who willingly
offered himself unto the Lord; and with him two hundred thousand mighty men of valor."

With commanding skill and steady march of logical
array, though at greater length than some might think
desirable to-day, he imbues his hearers with the sentiments of religion and sketches for them the principles involved in the voluntary organization of men into society,
in the sense of liberty and justice they must preserve,
in the spirit of service and sacrifice they must be prepared
to render each other. He shows how these are linked together and fused into power by the religious sentiment
when it pervades them.

"Firmly to believe," he says, "fully to realize, deeply
to be impressed with the great principles of piety to God,
to act as under his immediate inspection and as accountable
to him for every step, . . . must have the happiest tendency to store the mind with the noblest sentiments and
lead a man to act with the firmest resolution and most
exalted views."

Then, after creating this profoundly religious atmos-
phere, he takes the soldier virtue and sets it on the pedestal
of a great definition. "Valor, or true fortitude, is that
virtue by which men are enabled to preserve presence of
mind, to possess themselves fully, think clearly, judge
wisely, and act with firmness and calmness and resolution
in times of great confusion and tumult, in the midst of most
pressing dangers and perplexing distresses. . . . True
valor is a moral virtue, having reason for its foundation
and religion for its encouragement and support."

Thus does he exalt the character of the soldier. He

was arguing on the basis of beliefs that might not seem sufficient to-day, but they won ready assent and stirred the motives of his hearers then. He presented them by a method that would seem needlessly deliberate, and perhaps at times long drawn out, but it was the method that took effect. An hour and a half of rigorous thinking had a pleasurable zest to the unjaded minds of that day.

The spirit of this occasion into which I have sought sympathetically to enter makes one feel that this was a real occasion and that men were being moulded by the thoughts they heard. In modern times he who invents the finer rifle may win the next war. This country parson was fashioning his hearers into an instrument of power, imbuing their spirits with a re-enforcement of utmost value in the crisis when men are wont to fail. He was tempering their spirits by the magnitude of the motives with which he plied them. It was in 1768: he was planting the harvest of 1775.

Another scene illustrates our theme. It is later by seven years. Three men are seated together. One wears homespun, is a stocky man, with firm-set features, positive and intense. Another is more richly clothed, with embroidered waistcoat and signs of wealth upon him, refined in feature, urbane in manner, courteous in speech. The third is our parson, in his clerical garb, with a face that shows the power to think broadly, to speak to a purpose, and to act wisely.

These three men are in council. A price is on the heads of two of them, and the third is yoke-fellow with them through his protecting courage. It is true there was a natural kinship represented in this household, the wife of one of them being cousin to a third. But a deeper reason bound them together,—the kinship of a great cause. It was no association merely of family convenience. These men came together time after time and conferred on the great themes of government and justice, on the prospect of throwing off oppression if it were unduly manifest, and on nation building, on the rights of revolution and the intricate questions of wisdom and policy involved, until they knew their common mind, to which each one had contributed his share.

The world knows that two of these men were leaders in the movement out of which a nation was born. I believe it true that these two would not have been so effective as they were without the third. They were drawn together by mutual helpfulness and worth, and their names should stand together when we remember the cause for which they wrought,—Hancock and Adams and Clarke!

It has sometimes been questioned why the War of the Revolution began in Lexington. There were several miles between here and Charlestown. There were other reasons indeed, but part of the reason was Jonas Clarke. The spirit of this triumvirate had been disseminated by him with peculiar forcefulness until the men who had come under his immediate influence were prepared to sense the crisis when it arose and to act wisely and yet without reserve. The martyr spirit shown on yonder green was no impulse of the moment, but it was the deliberate witness of matured conviction, grounded in a spirit of devotion that was already ripe for sacrifice. And the fostering priest was Jonas Clarke. Such was he as counsellor and inspirer in the great cause.

Upon the third scene I cannot enter with any hope to do it justice. It was in 1781; and now Mr. Clarke is addressing His Excellency the Governor, the Lieutenant Governor, the honorable Council, the Senate and House of Representatives. It was the first day of general election after the adoption of the Constitution and the establishment of this Commonwealth as an independent State. He applies the exalted imagery of the Psalms to the men

before him. The rulers of the people,—they are the
shields of the earth, and they belong to God. By his customary method he weaves together principles pertinent
to the occasion: civil government is a necessity; all men
by nature are free, equal, and independent in this matter.
"It is in compact, in compact alone, that all just government is founded."

The principle of pure democracy is near to his heart,
and he is jealous to awaken the sense of responsibility in
the people as well as to secure for them their rights. In
one strong passage he shows by comparison with Rome
how the ultimate power is vested in the people:—

"When Brutus, the elder, greatly dared to attempt a
radical revolution from an arbitrary to a free government
by the expulsion of the Tarquins and the establishment
of a commonwealth at Rome, the virtue of his fellow-citizens seconded and supported him, and the glorious plan
was carried to effect to the inexpressible joy of every friend
to liberty, to his country, and to the rights of mankind.
But when, from the same patriotic principles, Brutus, the
younger, by the death of Julius Cæsar several ages afterward, nobly attempted the deliverance of his country
from the shackles of tyranny and the oppressor's yoke and
to re-establish a free government, the virtue of his fellow-
citizens failed him, and Rome was enslaved, never, never
to enjoy the blessings of liberty or a free government more!
And this was her choice."

So he impresses upon those rulers of the people the power
that evermore is vested in the people themselves, and he
says that rulers are accountable to the people. Then,
the other side, he brings home to them the deep obligation
coming from this fact, that they also still belong to God.
"All men by nature are free and equal in this matter."
"Civil rulers belong to God." "They are to fear God—
hate covetousness—shake their hands from bribes—to

judge righteously—to be no respecters of persons in judgment—not to be afraid of the face of man, but always to realize that the judgment is God's."

Having helped to form the State and being most solicitous about the Constitution, an early copy of which is closely annotated in his own hand, showing the suggestions and the changes that he would have liked to make, especially in the interest of religious liberty and sectarian freedom, he maintained an unabated interest to insure its integrity and perpetuity. Well might he exult in solemn gladness over the issue as he reviews the then recent past. A series of oppressive measures and lawless claims of arbitrary power, adopted and pursued by the court of Great Britain, in open violation of the most sacred chartered rights; arms to enforce obedience; and the power of the British legislature to make laws, binding on the colonies in all cases whatsoever, being openly assumed and declared,—roused and raised the spirit of liberty in the free-born sons of America to the highest pitch. And, no alternative being left them but the sword or slavery, these colonies hesitated not a moment, but unitedly declared their choice of the former and "greatly dared to be free."

"The important die was cast and the glorious era of liberty commenced. All America heard the alarm. To Heaven the appeal was made. By Heaven the claim was supported. That God who sitteth upon the throne of his holiness the Governor among the nations, . . . hath plead our cause and maintained our right to freedom, equality and independence, and given us a name among the nations of the earth."

These words and others similar to them are familiar to us to-day. They have entered into the vocabulary of our American thought. These phrases as penned by Jonas Clarke, often reproduced in his sermons, show that he was helping to form the thinking of the people by fashioning for them the instruments they used. These words, I say, are familiar to us to-day; but think of the import they had when uttered six years after the Revolution had begun, at the inauguration of the life of this Commonwealth. Think of how they re-enforced the already strong determination of these noble men who constituted that body of our legislature.

These three occasions are typical of the influence which Jonas Clarke was exerting in his day. They are not isolated ones, but are part and substance of what he was continually doing throughout those perilous and critical times. I seek not unduly to exalt him, surely not to overestimate his work, but simply to recognize the service he rendered and to accord to him the honor that is his due. It will be unquestioned that he was a man of large calibre, of comprehensive mind and forceful thought, of unremitting devotion to the cause of liberty in the State and nation he loved so well.

In the text there is one word that fittingly gives him his place. "Walk about Zion, and go round about her: tell the towers thereof. Mark ye well her bulwarks, consider her palaces; that ye may tell it to the generation following." Jonas Clarke, minister and patriot, was a veritable *bulwark* of the State and nation. We honor ourselves as we commend his character and service, telling it to the generation following.

EXTRACTS FROM LETTER OF MISS BETTY CLARKE, DAUGHTER OF REV. JONAS CLARKE.

[This letter, written by Miss Betty Clarke to her niece, Mrs. Lucy Ware Allen, of Northborough, Mass., was found among Mrs. Allen's papers in the old Allen parsonage at Northborough, in 1907, by Mrs. Allen's grand-daughter, Mrs. Harriet H. Johnson, and was by her presented to the Lexington Historical Society. The extracts here printed were read by the Corresponding Secretary before the society at its February, 1908, meeting.]

LEXINGTON, April 19th 1841, *not* 1775.

My dear niece Lucy Allen:

Miss Cotton offers to take a line to you, and, as your little girl did not stay or come to this house only to give us your letter which, with the sincerest joy we read and have lived on the hope you gave us that you would come up to this old House and look on us old Beings, a house and Happy, *Happy* home and many worthy men and women have been the Inhabitants and oh! Lucy, how many Descendants can I count from the venerable Hancock down to this day which is sixty six years since the war began on the Common which I now can see from this window as here I sit writing, and can see, in my mind, just as plain, all the British Troops marching off the Common to Concord, and the whole scene, how Aunt Hancock and Miss Dolly Quinsy, with their cloaks and bonnets on, Aunt Crying and ringing her hands and helping Mother Dress the children, Dolly going round with Father, to hide Money, watches and anything down in the potatoes and up Garrett, and then Grandfather Clarke sent down men with carts, took *your* Mother and all the children but Jonas and me and Sally a Babe six months old. Father sent Jonas down to Grandfather Cook's to see who was killed and what their condition was and, in the afternoon, Father, Mother with me and the Baby went to the Meeting House, there was the eight men that was killed, seven of them my Father's parishoners, one from Woburn, all in Boxes made of four large Boards Nailed up and, after Pa had prayed, they were put into two horse carts and took into the grave yard where your Grandfather and some of the Neighbors had made a large trench, as near the Woods as possible and there we followed the bodies of those *first slain, Father, Mother*, I and the Baby, there I stood and there I saw them let down into the ground, it was a little rainey but we waited to see them Covered up with the Clods and then for fear the British should find them, my Father thought some of the men had best Cut some pine or oak bows and spread them on their place of burial so that it looked like a heap of *Brush*.

Now, dear Lucy, only think that the hand who holds the pen to relate the above, did six years ago, see them same bodies gathered up, placed in a hansom Coffin with Urns, the names of the Eight men that was killed that Morn, and again buried in a hansome tomb made by the side of the Monument where they are now to remain untill they are called by the *Last Trumpett* to take their Last Rest in Heaven.

The extraordinary circumstance that I should be the only one of this Family who should witness the first Burial of the first slain of the war between Great Britain and America and Be not only continued in Life but on the same spot of Earth and in the same house where the first Patriots in the Country was at that period, Hancock and Adams and Father who was known as a superior *Wigg*, superior minister, a Highly respectable Man, uncommon in his intellectual faculties and, above all, a *Christian*, who served his Lord and Master, was faithfull to his People, gave his strength to labour for his Family, his hours of Rest to his pen so that his People's souls should not be neglected, but Lucy, I shall tire you with my relations, many, many sorrowful relations in this my long Life I could relate but I will also say I have had many years of comfort and, formerly, had good society and great assistance. Many are Dead, many have fallen off, *but*, BUT, God's name be praised, some are still left for my comfort and assistance. My dearest and *most* constant, *most* true, most considerate are from the Descendants of my oldest sister, Mary, and the VERY BEST of Men Her Husband.

Now, you will read this incoherent scrawl from your Aged Aunt who has suffered more sorrow and grief the *two* years past than she ever did in the seventy six years before. If ever we meet I shall gladly embrace you as one of my comforts, assistants in every care and labour, in my perplexities, in a great many scenes goyous as well as Grevious, which I hold in Gratefull remembrance, for I am truly thankfull to God that he has continued to me my memory that I am able to call to mind the Merceys and the great care he has taken of me when great dangers have surrounded.

I think of so many things that I Gumble them up in such bad writing that you will have hard work to read, my hands tremble and my Eyes are very sore lately, do pray read with patience perhaps my Last Letter for I am full of years and my two Last has caused me to wish to die (at times). But pray to live to see how the endless confusion of this Place will end.

(Signed)   YOUR AGED AUNT ELIZA.

SAMUEL ADAMS.*

By James P. Munroe. Read February 11, 1908.

We very properly call Washington the Father of his Country; but the real founder of these United States was not Washington, it was Samuel Adams. It is doubtful if we could have won in the Revolutionary War without the lofty courage and wise generalship of Washington. It is doubtful if the United States could have weathered the still harder period following the Revolution, had it not been for the strength and wisdom of the first President. But it is also doubtful if we should have had a Revolutionary War at all,—and therefore a field for Washington's great qualities,—had it not been for the tireless efforts and the extraordinary skill and power of Samuel Adams, who, John Fiske says, should stand second only to Washington as the greatest of Americans. Boston led the movement against the arbitrary rule of Great Britain; but it was Samuel Adams who led Boston. Boston stirred up Massachusetts and the other colonies to resist taxation; but it was Samuel Adams who stirred up Boston. And he did this not by eloquence and fiery speech-making, —for he was no orator: he stirred up Boston, he stirred up Massachusetts, he stirred up all the colonies by letters to the newspapers, by correspondence, voluminous and fiery, most of all by resolutions passed in that greatest political institution which America ever possessed or ever will possess,—the New England town-meeting.

It is superfluous to describe the principles and methods

* As this paper was first read at the Old South Meeting-house in Boston, which was so largely the forum for Adams's activities, it seems fitting to leave the references to that building unchanged. The reader has only to imagine himself within its storied walls.— J. P. M.

of the town-meeting; but perhaps we do not always remember what a perfect instrument for the teaching and preservation of democracy that town-meeting has been and still is, and how much the city youth and man loses in not having an opportunity to watch the machinery of government, to debate public questions, and to interrogate, face to face, the officials under whose rule he lives. I have no hesitation in saying that the moulders of America have been, not its presidents, governors, and other great dignitaries, but those humble though powerful officials called Moderators, who are sworn to show no favor in conducting the town-meetings, and who must let the meanest and poorest citizen express his views as freely and lengthily as he chooses, provided only he keeps within hailing distance of the question before the house.

One hundred and fifty years ago, however, the towns in Massachusetts were more democratic than they are to-day; for the people of that time not only settled, in their town-meetings, all such questions as they do at present, they also decided who should be the minister and how much (or, rather, how little) salary he should be paid. As a consequence, the citizens grew into the habit of discussing all kinds of questions about church-government, morals, and religion, and were accustomed, therefore, to look at every civic and political problem from its ethical as well as from its material side. But there was still another function exercised by those old town-meetings which has long since passed into oblivion,—that of taking direct part in the work of the General Court. For in those earlier days the legislature was regarded by the towns of Massachusetts simply as a sort of joint town-meeting, and the representatives sent to the General Court were instructed by formal resolutions of the town how they should vote on all important questions.

These facts are essential to an understanding of the

action of the colonies in the ten or twelve years before the
battle of Lexington,—the facts that the people at that
time had been educated by one hundred and twenty-five
years of town-meetings to manage their own affairs through
the most perfect form of democratic government ever
devised; that those colonial meetings were practically
free from all supervision by the British government;
that those town gatherings considered not only the affairs
of daily life, but also great moral questions; and that
they took an active part in the business of the whole
commonwealth by instructing their representatives to
the General Court how to vote upon every large question
affecting the whole colony.

I have said that the towns of Massachusetts were perfect democracies; but I should have excepted Boston.
There was a world of difference between the town governments of Massachusetts and the superimposed colonial
rule; and Boston, as the seat of his Majesty's government for Massachusetts, was filled with Crown officers,
with military men, with rich merchants having intimate
relations with the mother country, and with younger sons
of the nobility sent over here to make a living. So in
Boston there was a large and very powerful aristocracy
wholly in sympathy with British rule; and the contest
there in the eleven years, 1764–75, was not only one
between the colonists and the mother country, but a
contest between democracy as represented by the town-
meeting and aristocracy as represented by most of the
wealthy merchants and conspicuous officials.

The Boston of that day did not rest mainly upon piles:
it was a narrow but solid peninsula extending out into the
harbor, and it possessed no houses higher than three stories.
Therefore, the few public buildings, such as Faneuil Hall,
the Old State House, and the Old South Meeting-house,
loomed up as prominent objects visible from everywhere.

Metaphorically, too, those three buildings stand forth as great landmarks in American history, for in one or the other of them took place almost all the famous scenes of the opening of the Revolutionary War.

In one end of the Old State House met the Provincial Assembly, or General Court, and at the other end met the governor and his council. In Faneuil Hall assembled the ordinary town-meetings of Boston; but, when there was any particularly exciting meeting,—and there were many in those ten years before 1775,—Faneuil Hall was not big enough; so they would adjourn to this Old South Meeting-house, and the thousands of over-wrought townspeople would come sweeping up through what are now Adams Square and Washington Street, and would surge into this building until every corner upon the floor and in the galleries was filled.

In this old town where everybody knew everybody else, and in those lively old town-meetings where everybody felt free to speak his mind, Samuel Adams played his great part as the stirrer-up and leader of the Revolution.

Samuel Adams was not born a poor boy, though he was always a poor man. His father was one of the leading citizens of Boston, and his grandfather was brother to the grandfather of John Adams. Samuel was born in 1722 in a good house on Purchase Street, with a beautiful garden stretching down to the harbor and having a fine view of Massachusetts Bay. The boy went to Harvard, was graduated when he was eighteen, and wanted to study law; but law wasn't considered a very respectable occupation in those days, so his parents forbade it, and tried to turn a man who would have been a wonderfully good advocate into what proved to be a very unsuccessful merchant. The young man had no taste for this, kept losing money and losing more money, until, finally, with the little that was left he and his father set up a malt-house in

their garden on Purchase Street. This was fairly successful for a while; but that was not considered very respectable, either, and in later years Adams's enemies took great
pleasure in calling him "Sam the Maltster."

Probably the main reason why the Adamses—father and
son—did not succeed better in a material way was because
they were far more interested in town affairs than in their
own concerns. We find Samuel Adams serving on many
town committees and as moderator of town-meetings for
a number of years; but, singularly enough, he did not become really prominent until he was forty-two. In those days
a man of that age was considered venerable, and Adams,
moreover, carried out that view, for his hair was quite
gray and he had a trembling of the head and hands which,
while it added impressiveness to his public speaking, made
him seem much older than he was. He had been contributing letters to the newspapers for a number of years,—
the kind of letter signed *Veritas*, *Senex*, etc., which made up
the greater substance of those pre-Revolutionary journals,—
but his first writing of consequence was a document prepared for a town-meeting, a document which was adopted,
protesting against the proposed Stamp Act. This paper
is important in being the first formal statement ever
made by the colonies that Parliament had no right to
tax them and in containing the very first suggestion that
the colonies get together to secure redress.

In the fall of that year, 1764, he was elected a member
of the Provincial Assembly, or General Court, and almost
immediately he—together with James Otis—became the
leader in those stirring times. In the following May
(1765) Adams was re-elected to the General Court, the
other three members from Boston being Thomas Cushing
(long-time Speaker of the House), John Hancock, and
James Otis. At this session Adams was elected Clerk of
the House, and the annual salary of £100 was about all

that he and his family had to live on for a number of years.

Meanwhile the Stamp Act had been repealed; but the British government, pretending to believe that it was the kind of tax, not the fact of being taxed, that the colonies objected to, proposed to put other taxes upon paper, glass, painters' colors, and tea. Worse than that, however, they proposed to use the money from these taxes for giving regular salaries to the governors, judges, and other officers appointed by the king, who heretofore had been dependent upon the votes of the Provincial Assemblies. This the colonies did not like at all, and every manner of wild suggestion was advanced. A sensible plan of resistance, however, and one that met with popular favor was made by Samuel Adams, that the colonists should stop importing English goods and should establish manufactures of their own. At his suggestion town-meetings were held throughout Massachusetts to arouse the people against using British goods and to encourage the starting of domestic industries.

The Massachusetts Assembly prepared various documents, most of which Samuel Adams wrote, in relation to these taxes. Among them was a petition to the king, and, when Mr. Adams had finished writing it, his daughter said, "In a few weeks that paper will be touched by the royal hand." "More likely," replied her father, "it will be spurned by the royal foot." The document which made the most stir, however, was a so-called "Circular Letter," sent by the Massachusetts Assembly to the other colonies, urging them to work together and to devise some means of making the mother country listen to their complaints and grievances. This circular letter so angered the king and his ministers that they ordered Governor Bernard to dissolve the General Court and not to let it meet again until it should agree to withdraw the obnoxious letter. Not only did the General Court, before dissolving, vote not to withdraw the letter, but town-meetings were everywhere held upholding the members and making very vigorous protests against taxation without representation. The king's government, therefore, determined to break the spirit of the colonies by forbidding town-meetings, by having such leaders as Adams and Otis arrested, and by sending troops to overawe the people. When the mother country took such violent action as this, Adams foresaw that reconciliation would be impossible, and from that moment, he afterwards said, he began to work night and day for the absolute independence of America.

Since the General Court would not rescind the Circular Letter, since it could not meet again until it did, and since it was important for the towns to confer, the Boston town-meeting, at Adams's suggestion, got around the difficulty by calling a conference, in Boston, of town representatives. To this invitation ninety-six towns responded; and, while they did not accomplish much, they found out how easy it was to get together, and the time was rapidly approaching when they would need to act in unity. For on the very day (in October, 1768) that this convention adjourned, the two famous regiments (the fourteenth and twenty-ninth) arrived in Boston for the purpose of frightening the rebellious inhabitants into good behavior.

The year 1769 was devoted by most of the people of Boston to abusing equally the importers of English goods and these imported English soldiers. Both were hooted at and called all manner of evil names continually, and the town government and the governor were in a ceaseless quarrel over quarters for the troops. The town said that the soldiers should be kept down at the Castle (where Fort Independence now stands), but the governor declared that for the protection of himself and the other Crown officers they should be kept on duty in the very midst of the town. So the streets and the Common resounded with drums and marching, and the main guard was posted on King (now State) Street, with guns pointed at the Assembly Chamber. Considering the way they were abused by the tongues of the townspeople, the soldiers behaved pretty well; and, of course, the longer they refrained from using force, the more abusive the populace became. Therefore, it is a matter for wonder that not until they had been in Boston a year and a half did a real clash between the "lobster backs" and the citizens take place. That clash, needless to say, was the Boston Massacre, in which three citizens were killed and one mortally wounded.

That affray took place in the evening. Early the next morning the citizens, wild with indignation, assembled at Faneuil Hall in town-meeting, and appointed a committee of fifteen, with Hancock as chairman, to interview the governor and tell him that the regiments must be sent away. The meeting then adjourned till three o'clock in the afternoon, while the committee should wait upon Governor Hutchinson. He told them, as he had repeatedly said before, that he had no power to order the removal of the troops. The committee were so determined, however, and the crowds in the streets were so threatening, that Hutchinson at last agreed to remove the twenty-ninth regiment, which had been concerned in the Massacre, to the Castle in the harbor. He absolutely refused, however, to order away the fourteenth.

Meanwhile the town-meeting had again assembled, and the people, pouring in from the surrounding towns at the news of the Massacre, had so swelled the numbers that Faneuil Hall would not hold half the crowd. So the meeting was adjourned to this Old South Meeting-House. Imagine the streets between here and Faneuil Hall filled with a tremendously excited crowd, and hear the cry, "Make way for the Committee of Fifteen," as that committee, with Hancock and Adams at their head, emerge from the Old State House with the governor's answer, and squeeze their way towards the waiting town-meeting. As the committee pass through the human lane which is made for them, Adams leans from one side to the other, repeating, in a stage whisper, "Both regiments or none," "Both regiments or none." Arrived at the Old South, the report is made that the governor will remove the twenty-ninth but will not remove the four-teenth regiment. Then the people, understanding what Adams meant, give a great shout,—"Both regiments or none"; and the meeting votes tumultuously that a Com-mittee of Seven should go back to the governor with this ultimatum of the town. Day had begun to wane, and in the dim firelight of the Council Chamber sat the governor and his advisers, together with Colonel Dalrymple, the commander of the troops, waiting for the people's mes-sage; and here in this high, gloomy church sat the people, waiting for the governor's reply.

It was a great moment in Samuel Adams's life when he strode into the Council Chamber ready to tell Governor Hutchinson that the will of the people must override the orders of the king. You know that picture of him in Faneuil Hall,—that picture painted by Copley, which represents Adams at this moment standing with his head thrown back, determination on every line of his face, his right hand crushing a roll of manuscript and his left hand outstretched, pointing to the Massachusetts Charter. And these are some of the words that he boldly said, knowing that every word meant rebellion, and rebellion hanging:—

"If you, or Colonel Dalrymple under you, have the power to remove one regiment, you have the power to remove both; and nothing short of their total removal will satisfy the people or preserve the peace of the Province. A multitude highly incensed now wait the result of this application. The voice of ten thousand freemen demands that both regiments be forthwith removed. Their voice must be respected, their demand obeyed. Fail not then at your peril to comply with this requisition. On you alone rests the responsibility of this decision; and, if the just expectations of the people are disappointed, you must be answerable to God and your country for the fatal consequences that must ensue."

A long discussion followed; and, finally, Hutchinson, urged by his counsellors and even by Dalrymple, gave in, and the message was brought back to the waiting people that democracy had won. Within a week both regiments were removed to the Castle; and always afterwards they were called the "Sam Adams Regiments."

Adams and democracy had for the moment triumphed, but the next two years were years of reaction. Times grew hard and harder, New York, which had agreed to the non-importation of British goods, went back on this agreement and so broke the force of the whole plan, the king's government grew more and more determined, the Whigs of Boston more and more discouraged, and the Tories, consequently, more and more confident. In this crisis Adams saw that the only way to strengthen the cause of independence would be to bring the force of all the Massachusetts town-meetings to bear upon the somewhat wavering policies of the Boston town-meeting. Therefore, in the fall of 1772 he moved, in the Boston meeting, that "a committee of Correspondence be appointed, to consist of twenty-one persons, to state the rights of the colonists, and of this Province in particular, as men and Christians and as subjects; and to communicate and publish the same to the several towns and to the world," etc. Most of his friends thought this plan rather absurd, and many of them refused to serve on the committee; but the response which came from the towns soon showed Adams to have been right. These committees, we now know, were the very mainsprings of the Federal Union. It is inspiring to read the bold words which came in to the Boston meeting during the winter of 1772–1773 from these towns. Said the people of Roxbury: "Our pious forefathers died with the pleasing hope that we, their children, should live free. Let none, as they will answer it another day, disturb the ashes of those heroes by selling their birthright." Ipswich advised that the "inhabitants should stand firm as one man to support and maintain all their just rights and privileges." Salisbury, Beverly, Lynn, Danvers, and Rowley declared for an American Union. And in Plymouth the vote showed that there were ninety to one ready, if need be, to fight Great Britain.

This action of Massachusetts spread to the other colonies, and in 1773 Virginia proposed that there be Committees of Correspondence between all the colonies. Later we shall see how Massachusetts responded to this suggestion; but meanwhile occurred an event that brought the colonies still closer together in their opposition to increasing tyranny. As a result of the non-importation agreements, the new taxes had yielded practically no revenue to the Crown. Therefore, they were now all taken off excepting the tax on tea, which was left in order to show that the king reserved the right to tax. We have not time to go into the long controversy over this new taxation question, or to rehearse the self-sacrifice of the American women in giving up their favorite beverage and in drinking catnip tea instead. You know how the shiploads of the proscribed herb were consigned to certain agents here, how those agents refused to resign, how the Boston town-meeting tried to induce Hutchinson to send the tea back, and how he would not. After the arrival of the first tea-ship, the "Dartmouth," on November 17, 1773, town-meetings were held almost daily,—most of them in this meeting-house,—resolutions that the tea never should be landed were passed, the ship was constantly guarded by armed citizens, and mounted couriers stood ready to alarm the country, should the tea be brought on shore. At last came the day when, by law, the tea must be landed by the customs officers. The owners were ready to send the cargoes back; but the customs officers would not give them permission, and two armed vessels were stationed in the channel with orders to sink the ships, should they try to leave without their clearance papers. This was the 16th of December. Couriers had gone all over the province with the news; people from the whole eastern part of Massachusetts had poured in to see what was going to happen; and a town-meeting called here was attended by seven thousand persons, who filled the meeting-house and spread through the surrounding streets. This assemblage gave the owner of the tea-vessel one more chance. So, in obedience to its orders, the much-abused man travelled way out to Hutchinson's country house on Milton Hill to beg once again for a permit to send his cargo back. Meanwhile the great crowd sat here till long after dark, with Samuel Adams on this platform as moderator, debating and discussing. Evidently, something was going to happen; but only the few in the secret knew just what. After a long time poor old Mr. Rotch came back from Milton, and reported that the governor had again refused him a permit. Immediately Mr. Adams arose, and in a loud and solemn voice said, "This meeting can do nothing more to save the country." That was the prearranged signal. Instantly a loud war-whoop was heard, and forty or fifty men disguised as Indians rushed by the door, down Milk and Purchase Streets to Griffin's Wharf, off which the tea-ships were moored. The crowd rushed after them, and such a tumult and howling quiet Boston had not heard for many a day. The imitation Indians were quiet enough, however, when they got on board the ship, and in a short time had hoisted every chest of tea, broken it open, and dumped the contents into the sea. This last desperate measure had been planned under the direction of Adams in a printing-office on Court Street, which was long a favorite meeting-place of the patriot leaders.

The king's answer to the Boston Tea Party was the Boston Port Bill. The English ministry thought this a very shrewd move; for, by closing the port of Boston to all entering and outgoing ships, the occupation of most of the people would be gone, and it was hoped that they would be starved into submission. Furthermore, by diverting trade from Boston, other towns and colonies would benefit and would make so much profit that, it was thought, they would be quite willing to desert rebellious Boston. But in this they were completely mistaken. Although, to get back her trade, all the Boston town-meeting had to do was to vote payment for the destroyed tea, they would not pass such a vote. The towns which might have profited by Boston's misfortune refused to do so. Money, provisions, and votes of praise and encouragement came in from all over the colonies; and the demand for a congress of all the colonies grew louder and louder.

In the interval the governor, practically powerless against the obstinacy of the Boston town-meeting, had asked for leave of absence and had gone over to England, General Gage being appointed governor in his place. As Boston was in disgrace, Gage forbade the General Court to meet here, and ordered it to Salem, where it convened in June, 1774. Its chief business was to appoint delegates to the proposed Continental Congress at Philadelphia; but this was kept a profound secret, for, had it been known, Gage would have dissolved the Assembly before it had a chance to carry out this plan. Samuel Adams, however, was equal to the emergency. Keeping the General Court busy with matters of not much consequence, and having it debate resolutions which looked as if Massachusetts were getting ready to yield to the king, he lulled suspicion to sleep, and meanwhile went about among the members, secretly pledging them to support him in what he proposed to do. At first he could be sure of only five members; but by the 17th of June (just a year before the battle of Bunker Hill) he was certain of a majority. So, as head of a committee on the state of the province, he suddenly brought in a resolve that five men whom he named should be appointed delegates to a colonial congress to be held at Philadelphia. The Tory members tried to choke off the measure and break up the session by leaving the hall; but Adams had had the doors locked and had pocketed the key. One member, however, did escape and carried the news of what was going on to Gage, who immediately sent his personal agent to dissolve the Assembly. But the Assembly refused to let the governor's messenger in until they had first passed a vote appointing the delegates, appropriated money for their expenses, and adopted various other measures against the government.

We have no time to take up the extraordinary history of those Continental Congresses which finally produced the Declaration of Independence and in which Samuel and John Adams and John Hancock played so conspicuous a part. But I would speak of still two more town-meetings which took place in this old meeting-house. The first was in June, 1774. Boston's trade was dead, her ships and wharves were rotting, grass was growing in her streets, men who had been rich were living on the charity of other towns, obstinacy seemed to have resulted in nothing, and a simple confession that the Tea Party had been wrong would restore her trade and industry. The Tories, therefore, thought this the right time to call a town-meeting at which to dissolve the Committee of Correspondence and to beg forgiveness of the mother country. Thousands came to the meeting,—they had nothing else to do. Gloom was on every face, fear of the future in every heart. Continued resistance meant starvation and ruin. But Samuel Adams, leaving the chair as moderator, led the debate for hours, and, when the vote was finally taken, the townspeople, by a great majority, declared themselves determined to continue to resist. Moreover, they entered into a "solemn league and covenant" to use no British goods whatever until their wrongs should be righted. That was the crucial moment in Samuel Adams's long fight for the independence of the colonies. That vote of the Boston town-meeting meant ultimate war.

The second meeting was, like the first, illegal,—for town-meetings had been long ago forbidden,—and was held here on the 6th of March (the 5th being Sunday), 1775, the fifth anniversary of the Boston Massacre. The town was then wholly in the hands of soldiery,—there being eleven regiments stationed here,—a price was on the heads of Adams, Hancock, Otis, Warren, and the other patriot leaders, any clash between the military and the people meant riot, massacre, and the hanging of those patriot leaders. Yet here on this platform, behind a desk draped in mourning, calmly sat, as moderator of the meeting, Samuel Adams; and packed into every available inch of the room sat and stood the people, waiting for Joseph Warren, the orator, to appear. Scattered through the audience, to intimidate it, were many soldiers in uniform and armed. Observing them, Adams asked the townspeople to vacate the front rows, and invited the soldiers to occupy those pews, so that they might the better hear what Dr. Warren was about to say. A full hour beyond the appointed time that tense audience awaited Warren; and then he came in, not through the door, but through a window behind the pulpit, the crowd being so dense that he could find no other ingress. Warren was as eloquent as he was fearless, and every word he spoke was an invitation to the soldiers to cry treason and arrest him and the applauding audience. Indeed, one officer, sitting on the pulpit stairs, held up his open palm filled with bullets where all the audience could see. Warren, without a moment's hesitation, dropped his handkerchief over the bullets and went steadily on. What a scene that was; and how that and like scenes of that great time have made that Old South Meeting-house a sacred place forever!

I have spoken thus far mainly of Boston, for that was the headquarters of rebellion; but, each in its own way, every other town in Massachusetts was equally active. Take my own town of Lexington, for example. It had but seven hundred inhabitants, almost all of them plain farmers, many of them scarcely able to read or to write their names; but they knew history, they understood politics, they had been educated by a century of town-meetings to know their rights and to speak their minds. There was not an act of the Boston town-meeting or of the General Court which they had not eagerly followed; there had been no crisis in the affairs of the colony which had not had its Lexington town-meeting to discuss the matter and to instruct the town's representative. And that action was guided, those instructions were written, by one of the greatest patriots and keenest minds of that time of great men,—Parson Jonas Clarke, who for fifty years was minister of Lexington and whose sermons were trumpet calls to stand fast in the cause of liberty. Never was there a better school for patriots and a better teacher of the true principles of liberty than were those town-meetings of Lexington, and that leader in those meetings,— Parson Clarke.

It was no mere coincidence, therefore, that brought Hancock and Samuel Adams into Lexington on the 18th of April, 1775, and found them at the house of Parson Clarke on the very night that Gage had fixed upon to strike the first blow against the patriot cause. Hancock and Adams both had a high price on their heads: the very shadow of the gallows was over them; but they were serenely journeying to the second Continental Congress, sure that the people would protect them from all injury. And the inhabitants of Lexington were doing their part that night. For around Parson Clarke's house they had placed a guard of eight minute-men to keep careful watch. About midnight up came Paul Revere clattering, as history tells: there was a hurried conference between Revere, Hancock, and Adams; and, while the latter wanted to shoulder muskets and take part in the coming fight, they were persuaded that their lives were too precious to put in danger. Sergeant Munroe escorted them by back roads to a place of safety in Woburn, and got back to Lexington Green in time to line up the minute-men. As Adams started out across the hills in the first gray of the dawn, he is said to have exclaimed: "What a glorious morning for America!" It was indeed a glorious morning, and it meant the crowning of Samuel Adams's enormous labors during those eleven terrible years. From one point to another he had led the town-meetings until from humble petitioning they had gone on to proud defiance of the king, and at last had arrived at the place where they were ready to take up arms and to surrender their lives in defence of liberty.

Samuel Adams remained a conspicuous figure until his death in 1803. He took a leading part in all the Congresses of the Revolution and signed the Declaration of Independence. Moreover, it was he who prepared the Articles of Confederation. But from the opening of the Revolutionary War his influence and reputation seemed slowly to decline, so that not until comparatively recent years has his name begun to emerge from the sort of eclipse in which it rested behind those of such men as Washington, John Adams, and Jefferson. Why was this? Mainly, I think, because Samuel Adams had the abilities of a revolutionary rather than of a constructive statesman. He quite strenuously opposed, for example, the acceptance of the Constitution by the Massachusetts Convention, and only reluctantly agreed to its adoption when he perceived that further opposition would be vain. He was a Republican, moreover, in a State which at that time was overwhelmingly Federalist; yet, curiously enough, while the other Republicans had followed the free-thinking of Jefferson and Paine, he continued a stanch supporter of the strictest Calvinism. His absorption in politics, furthermore, had made him wholly neglectful of such lesser matters as the support of his family, and had induced a carelessness in money affairs which had laid him open to charges, unquestionably unfounded, of having, as tax-collector, misappropriated funds. Finally, his long years of fighting against British tyranny had made him, to use a good Yankee word, "cantankerous," and militated against his making those concessions to the views and opinions of others so essential in the building of a State. His election, therefore, in 1794, after he had served some years as lieutenant-governor, to the governorship of Massachusetts, was in the nature of a reward somewhat perfunctorily given, in recognition of his earlier services, rather than a spontaneous choice of the people. An appreciation of this fact, as well as the increasing infirmities of his seventy-five years, led him, therefore, in 1797 to decline a renomination. He passed the remaining six or seven years of his life sitting in his modest house or his pleasant garden in Winter Street, exchanging reminiscences with his contemporaries, fast thinning in number, or receiving the respectful homage of the younger generation.

On the domestic side the burden, ever since their early marriage, had been mainly carried by his excellent and devoted wife (who by her extraordinary thrift made up in some measure for his lack of it), and by his many friends, who had to go so far, sometimes, as to fit him out with such clothes and sums of money as he must have to make a decent appearance as a public man. His only son, Samuel, was graduated at Harvard in 1771, studied medicine with Dr. Joseph Warren, served as a surgeon throughout the Revolution, but received in that service such damage to his constitution that he died in 1788. The money received from the government as compensation for the services of this son was the sole support of Mr. Adams during his final years. It is interesting in this connection to remember that the very large sums left in charity, a few years ago, by Dr. John and Miss Belinda Randall, were derived almost wholly from the increment of that Adams property (they being grandchildren of Samuel Adams through his daughter) on Winter, Washington, and other down-town streets, which was of no contributory support to their illustrious grandfather.

Another descendant, Mr. William V. Wells, published some years ago a biography of his ancestor which fills three volumes, and which, it seems to me, tries to claim too much for Samuel Adams. He was a great figure—seemingly an indispensable figure—during the decade preceding the battle of Lexington; but his greatest work for his country ended on that April morning when he stood on the hills of Lexington and uttered (or might have uttered) that prophetic phrase. The Massachusetts town-meeting had done its noble work; and Samuel Adams, the Man of the Town Meeting, the man who never faltered, never lost courage, never failed in resourcefulness, who would neither accept bribes nor heed threats, the "Great Incendiary," as Hutchinson called him, in whose hands (as Hutchinson also declared) all the other men were but puppets,—that man up to that day had been the guiding spirit of all. His cousin, John Adams, once enthusiastically called him "the wedge of steel which split the knot of *lignum vitæ* that tied America to England." That is a true description of the part he played; and the force he used was the enormous democratic power of the New England town-meeting. Those meetings were the main strength of the colonies. It was they which brought these colonies together in a splendid union, it was they that held the States together through the terrible crisis of the Civil War; and we cannot have real democracy in our huge modern cities until we find some way of getting at the people themselves, as Sam Adams reached them face to face in the town-meetings of the Old South Meeting-house and Faneuil Hall.

ARCHITECTURAL YESTERDAYS IN LEXINGTON.

A FRAGMENTARY ACCOUNT OF SOME OF THE OLDER BUILDINGS AND THEIR BUILDERS.

By Dr. Fred Smith Piper. Read October 13, 1908.

It is the purpose of this paper to give a brief sketch of some of the more conspicuous buildings and bits of architecture of former days in our town, accompanying numerous photographs.

There were many comfortable homes and some useful public buildings, but comparatively few specimens of meritorious style.

The inhabitants of those days had little means for luxury or show. They were industrious and prudent, and their buildings were in harmony with their lives. In a large measure the homes of people express their habits of thought and conditions of living. The local builders were not much inclined to the ornate, but rather favored economy and utility, and probably in most instances there was no architect other than the carpenter.

There were no brick buildings in town a century ago, and the gambrel roof, quite common in some localities, seldom appeared in Lexington.

The earliest houses in town of which we have any exact knowledge were the Bowman house, near Arlington Heights, and the Tidd house, near the north section of Hancock Street. The Bowman house is said to have been built in 1649, but this early date has been questioned, as it is within the decade of the very first permanent settlement in present territory of Lexington. It was a two-story wooden building, about forty feet on the front by

TIDD HOUSE.

HOUSE AT NO. 167 MASSACHUSETTS AVENUE

thirty feet on the ends, and had a lean-to roof. The front door casing was not elaborate, but had well-chosen pilasters with appropriate caps enclosing a three-pane window above the door. In the lower story in front there were two windows on either side of the door, and on the second story there were five windows, the central window being directly over the door. The upper sash contained six panes and the lower sash nine panes of glass. The windows on the back part of the house had two sashes of six panes each. There was a back door at the rear of the easterly end of the house, and probably the front door was seldom opened, except on important occasions, such as a funeral or a call from the parson. There was but one chimney, and that was in the centre of the house. The front face of the chimney exposed above the roof presented a peculiar decorative panel. This house was built by Nathaniel Bowman, who came from Watertown, and was destroyed by fire April 1, 1905.

The Tidd house was similar to the Bowman house, though probably a little larger. The front door and the windows were much alike in the two houses, while the chimney of the Tidd house had a projecting decoration in place of the panel of the Bowman chimney. John Tidd came from Woburn, and built this house about 1686, according to Hudson, though tradition in the Tidd family sets the date nearer 1670. It was taken down in 1891, and some of the boards and timbers were used in repairing the Old Belfry, which was replaced on Belfry Hill that year.

Buckman Tavern, built about 1690, and Munroe Tavern, built about 1695, are wooden structures similar to the Bowman and Tidd houses, except that Buckman Tavern has a two-pitch hip roof.

It seems fair to take these structures as types of the more substantial and comfortable houses and wayside hostelries of the first century of our town.

Regarding the first parsonage, built by vote of the parish near Vine Brook, for the Rev. Benjamin Estabrook, no reliable information can be found.

The small, original Hancock house, built about 1698 by Rev. John Hancock, and the Dr. Joseph Fiske house, built about 1732, are the best-known gambrel roofs. The one extravagant and notable feature about the Hancock House was the many-panelled front door.

While there are some beds of clay in Lexington, there seem to be none suitable for bricks or pottery. At one time there was a small pottery in East Lexington, but the clay was brought from Cambridge. (See Lexington Hist. Soc. Proceedings, vol. ii. p. 28.)

In 1828 the brick store on Massachusetts Avenue, opposite Pleasant Street, was built, the brick-work being done by Jacob Robinson, an uncle of our late Governor George D. Robinson. The store was owned by Mr. Eli Robbins, and was probably the first brick building in town. About this same time, or previous to 1833, Nathaniel Harrington built the brick house on Massachusetts Avenue opposite Lexington Green. It originally had a hip roof, which was replaced by the present Mansard roof in 1874. So far as ascertained, these were the only brick buildings in town up to the erection of the present town hall in 1871. (Dedicated April 19, 1871.)

Probably no estate along our main thoroughfare presents more dignity and apparent comfort than the home of Miss Dana (No. 139 Massachusetts Avenue). This house was built soon after 1800 by Obadiah Parker, who was proprietor of a private school on Pleasant Street (see Lexington Hist. Soc. Proceedings, vol. ii. pp. 33–35), but was never occupied till purchased by Miss Dana's grandfather, Ambrose Morell. (See Lexington Hist. Soc. Proceedings, vol. ii. p. 31, also pp. 179–186.) Mr. Parker also built the house next east of Miss Dana's residence, and had his

DANA HOUSE

STONE BUILDING

residence there for a period. The original structure of the Dana house was rather long and narrow, with brick ends, and the longest measurement fronting the street. It had a pitch roof with gables toward the east and the west.

Mr. Morell married Sally Holbrook of Sherburne, January 7, 1805, when she was eighteen years old, and they began their residence here on their wedding-day. They had four daughters,—Sarah, Clara, Elizabeth, and Mary. Elizabeth became the wife of Otis H. Dana and the mother of our esteemed Miss Ellen Dana.

The house was renovated in 1839, and fashioned substantially as it appears to-day. The changes in the house and the laying out of the garden were largely planned by Mrs. Sarah Millet, Mrs. Dana's oldest sister, and were probably suggested by estates which she had seen along the Hudson River. Curtis Capell was the carpenter in charge of the work. A new roof with overhanging gable toward the street was built. Four Greek Ionic columns, two feet in diameter at their bases, and placed at equal distances apart, adorn the front and give support to the gable. The shafts of these columns were constructed in Lexington, but the capitals were carved in Boston. Probably the front windows in the lower story were enlarged and brought down to the floor, and a new front door and frame built at this same time. Two tall chimneys rising from each brick end of the house mark the positions of the original fireplaces. The whole construction was so well planned and executed that no one to-day would suspect so great a transformation.

In 1833 Eli Robbins built the Stone Building, so called to-day, in East Lexington, to provide a public hall for lectures and entertainments in that part of the town. It must be remembered that the East Village was a very thrifty portion of Lexington at this period, having several manufactories, probably giving employment to one hundred or more men. (See Lexington Hist. Soc. Proceedings, vol. ii. p. 175.) John Colby was the contractor for the building, and Isaac Melvin was the architect. Mr. Colby employed on this building, among others, Isaac Buttrick, Curtis Capell, and a man by the name of Page. Page is said later to have become an architect of considerable ability, located in New York. Buttrick and Capell remained in Lexington, and both lived on Pleasant Street. Colby is remembered as a fine workman, but possessed of doubtful character and addicted to dissipation.

The history of the Stone Building (see Lexington Hist. Soc. Proceedings, vol. ii. p. 144) records a remarkable list of men who have lectured, preached, taught the youth, or sojourned within its walls:—Charles Follen, Ralph Waldo Emerson, Theodore Parker, Samuel J. May, A. Bronson Alcott, John S. Dwight, John Pierpont.

Architecturally, the building is unpretentious, but substantial and pleasing. The front gable projects beyond the body of the structure, and is well supported by four massive Doric columns. The gable contains two quarter-circle windows with finely wrought, radiating sash. The front door is somewhat ornate and a little distracting by its inharmonious lines.

This appears to have been Mr. Melvin's first work as an architect and Mr. Capell's first work as a carpenter in Lexington, but to each further reference will be made. Mr. Melvin boarded for a time in the house on the easterly corner of Massachusetts Avenue and Pleasant Street, now owned by Dr. Francis H. Brown and occupied by Mrs. Butterfield, and while there he remodelled the front door into its present beautiful form, judged by many to be the handsomest old-time door-way in town. Mr. Page, before mentioned as a workman on the Stone Building, later became a partner of Mr. Melvin's, but the dates of partnership are obscure.

FOLLEN CHURCH

Ground was broken for the foundation of Follen Church on the 4th of July, 1839. Dr. Charles Follen, the minister of the little parish, prepared the plans, and a Mr. Catrell of Cambridge was master builder. (See Lexington Hist. Soc. Proceedings, vol. ii. p. 151.)

The church is a unique octagonal auditorium with vestibule and spire on the central front. The base of the spire forming the vestibule is rectangular to the height of the main structure. Above this is an octagonal section having panels in the lower half, and lattice windows in the upper portion designating the position of the bell. The spire terminates in an octagonal pyramid, surmounted by a vane. The pulpit is directly opposite the entrance, and the organ and choir are immediately back of the pulpit.

This church was dedicated on January 15, 1840, and stands to-day as a modest reminder of the true and noble man whose name it bears.

Curtis Capell, the carpenter, was born in Groton, November 17, 1806, and had worked in Concord before coming to Lexington in May, 1832. He had a brother Thomas who was also a carpenter, but his father's business is unknown. Besides his work already mentioned, he built the Universalist church in East Lexington, which later became the first Catholic church in the town and is now known as Village Hall. He also built the residences now occupied by Mr. E. P. Nichols, Mr. Alex. Wilson, Mr. Charles Brown, and Mrs. Mitchell.

During this period of prosperity in East Lexington (1830 to 1850) a goodly number of comfortable homes were built, and on some of these we find evidences to-day of fine workmanship, particularly in the front doors and their frames.

Mr. Capell married May 2, 1832, Mary A. Brown. He died in Lexington, May 5, 1881, and is buried in Lexington Cemetery.

The old Town Hall, later high school, was built by David A. Tuttle in 1846 according to plans drawn by Isaac Melvin, architect, at a price of five thousand dollars above the cellar. There was a disagreement among the members of the building committee regarding a one-story or a two-story building, and the structure, as built, was a compromise, consisting of a two-story central portion with one-story extensions on either side. The front gable of the two-story part projected several feet, and was supported by four Roman Ionic columns, resting on hewn granite bases and arranged with about double the space between the two centre columns that there was between the central and side columns. The windows contained thirty panes of glass each, and, in harmony with the front door, were semicircular at the top. The front corners of the main part of the building were finished as pilasters with capitals like those on the columns. The façade was quite Roman in appearance, and was purposely copied to a degree as a decorative feature on the front and ends of the new high school erected in 1902, Cooper & Bailey, architects.

On the 23d of March, 1846, the First Parish voted that "the building committee proceed forthwith to make contracts for wheeling around and remodelling the meeting house agreeably to a plan by Mr. Isaac Melvin this day submitted." This, you will remember, was the third church in town, which was originally built in 1794 and the first to have a belfry. The committee contracted with Mr. S. B. Temple for the work of reconstruction. On December 7, 1846, the parish voted to furnish seats for the vestry, and chose a committee of three to install an organ at a cost not to exceed $1,200. The work of renovation was nearly complete, when the building was destroyed by fire on December 17, 1846. Parenthetically, it is interesting to notice that Rev. Jason Whitman was installed July 30, 1845, at a salary of nine hundred dollars.

OLD HIGH SCHOOL BUILDING

OLD BRICK STORE

It is also interesting to read in the parish records of a transaction not unlike present-day politics: On February 16, 1846, thirty-five members voted in favor of removing the church to the "Bowen Harrington lot," and thirty-one voted against it. Later in the same meeting the location of the church was referred to a committee for further consideration, and twelve persons were admitted to parish membership. About three weeks later—on March 9—forty-one voted to keep the church on the old site on the Common, and thirty-one favored the Bowen Harrington lot. This vote, reversing the decision of the previous meeting, suggests a possible motive in admitting the twelve new members at that particular meeting, and it is well known what an animated contest often arises over the locating of a public building. The church which was burned was a plain wooden building, 66 x 42 feet, with pitch roof showing gables toward the east and west (*i.e.*, toward Buckman Tavern and Belfry Hill) and a belfry on the end toward Buckman Tavern. The pulpit was high in the centre of the north side, and there were entrances on each of the other sides. (See Lexington Hist. Soc. Proceedings, vol. i. pp. 27, 28.)

(Joseph Underwood was contractor for building this church of 1794. See Lexington Hist. Soc. Proceedings, vol. ii. p. 104.)

As before mentioned, this church burned on December 17, 1846, and on the 29th of December, 1846, the parish chose Benjamin Muzzey, Samuel Bridge, and Nathaniel Mulliken to be a committee to consider locating and building a new church.

Some question had arisen regarding the title of the First Parish to the old location on the Common, three other church organizations having been formed by this time, and on December 7, 1846, a committee was chosen by the parish to confer with the selectmen regarding the matter.

No report of this committee appears, but on February 1, 1847, the parish voted, eighteen for the Bowen Harrington lot, called "the Garden Lot," and seven in favor of the old location. Only twenty-five votes were cast regarding the location of the new church, where seventy-seven votes had been cast relative to the location for the old church less than one year before.

On February 15, 1847, it was voted to take a deed of the Bowen Harrington lot and to proceed forthwith to erect a church at a cost not exceeding eight thousand dollars. Benjamin Muzzey, Nathaniel Mulliken, Samuel Bridge, William Smith, and Oliver W. Kendall were chosen a building committee. February 27, 1847, voted to adopt the design drawn by Mr. Isaac Melvin in January, 1846, which was apparently the plan for remodelling the former church. On March 15, 1847, it was voted to adopt the "Roman design" presented to the meeting this day by Mr. Isaac Melvin, architect. A meeting was called for April 12, 1847, to see if the parish would appropriate more money, and it was voted that "the matter be left to the Building Committee, for them to act on the same as they shall deem most for the interest of the society." There is no record of any meeting from this time (April 12, 1847) till October 11, 1847, when votes were passed to procure carpeting, cushions for the pews, a new bell, and a new organ, the organ not to cost over twelve hundred dollars.

The minister of the parish, Rev. Jason Whitman, died in Portland, Me., January 25, 1848, and was buried from the Baptist church in Lexington, January 28, 1848. The new meeting-house was dedicated on February 23, 1848. "The pews were offered at auction and a sufficient number were sold to pay the expense of erecting the new House" (Parish Records).

On October 19, 1848, George W. Robinson presented a "Gallery Clock."

An auditor having been chosen to examine the accounts of the building committee, he reported on March 31, 1851, as follows: A. P. Sherman took the contract for building the church for $8,567. Sundry expenses and services of the committee amounted to $1,315.66, making the total cost $9,882.66. No mention is made of the architect's fee. The receipts from the sale of pews amounted to $11,093.17. Commission of Isaac N. Damon for selling pews, $100. Balance to the credit of the parish, $1,110.51.

The auditorium of this meeting-house is 67' x 52' 6" floor measure, with walls 27' 10". The pulpit is in the centre of the northern end, while a small gallery, originally occupied by the organ and choir, is in the south end, overhanging the auditorium 9' 7", and extending over the vestibule 4' 3". An unoccupied room occupies the remainder of the space above the vestibule. A new three-manual organ, built by George S. Hutchings, was installed in 1898 in the rear of the pulpit, extending back into the vestry. After the introduction of the new organ, additional pews were built in the gallery. The auditorium has eight large windows, semicircular at the top. There are three windows on either side and one on each side of the vestibule in the south end.

The pulpit and exposed wood-work of the organ are mahogany, while the pews are native, old-growth pine, finished in mahogany stain and wax.

The auditorium is entered from a vestibule by three spacious doors. There are three aisles, one in the centre and one on either side, next to the side walls. The pews are arranged slightly curving toward the pulpit and in two double sections. The gallery is reached from the vestibule by stairs on either side.

Externally, the church consists of the body containing the auditorium, the porch and vestibule extending from the centre of the south end of the body, and the spire rising above the vestibule, all constructed of wood. The body is a plain rectangular structure, 77' 10" x 55' 6", clapboarded, and has a pitch roof rising at an angle of thirty-seven degrees. (Gable is 106 degrees.)

The vestibule extends twenty-four feet from the body of the church, and has a front of 29' 6". A balustrade above the cornice extends across the front and back on either side to the gable of the main structure.

A porch is formed by extending forward the roof and side walls of the vestibule about five feet beyond the front wall. The fronts of these projecting side walls are finished as square columns, and the corners of the body are finished as corner pilasters, all bearing capitals of Roman Ionic design. The porch is further supported and decorated by two Roman Ionic columns, 2' 6" in diameter at their bases, and resting upon blocks of granite. They are nearly nine feet apart and about six feet from either side column.

The entrance is by an ample door in the centre, framed by pilasters and cap in harmony with the finish elsewhere on the building.

The spire rises from the vestibule to a height of about a hundred and thirty feet above the ground. The base is twenty feet square, and, while plain in general effect, the severity is relieved by panels, which contain the clock dials, and by a pediment above. The second section of the spire is circular with four ornamental windows, whose frames, consisting of Corinthian pilasters and denticular cornice, project, giving the appearance of an octagon.

The third section is circular upon an octagonal drum, and contains eight windows. Each window has two sashes of six panes each, the top sash having semicircular heads. Between the windows are pilasters of the same style as seen on the section below, and a circular cornice above all. The terminal section is a gracefully tapering

SPIRE OF FIRST PARISH CHURCH

octagonal pyramid, supporting the points of compass and wind vane.

Just why the plan of this church is mentioned on the parish records as the "Roman design" is not apparent, but that the structure is beautiful and appropriate is generally agreed. The vestibule and porch, with its decorative columns and balustrade, extending five or six feet beyond the base lines of the spire on three sides, while the fourth side of the spire rests upon the gable of the main structure, lend beauty and distinction to this edifice beyond what is commonly seen in tall-spire churches. Exteriorly, it resembles the beautiful Arlington Street Church in Boston, but was built thirteen years earlier than the Boston church. (Arlington Street Church was built—corner-stone laid May 28, 1860. Plans were drawn by Gridley J. F. Bryant and Arthur Gilman.)

The present tower clock was purchased by popular subscription, chiefly through the enterprise of Mr. R. D. Blinn, and presented to the parish on November 22, 1869.

The bell is four feet in diameter at the base, and was cast by William Blake & Co. in 1872.

This church is often spoken of as a Christopher Wren style, but it has sufficient originality and artistic merit to honor the name of Isaac Melvin.

Mr. Melvin was born in Concord, on the road from Concord to Bedford and not far from the boundary between the two towns. His mother was Sally Mercer. He had a brother Thomas, and a sister who married a man by the name of Balcom. He came to Lexington about 1833, and removed to Cambridge some time during, or previous to, 1846. The records of the First Parish mention a parish meeting on February 16, 1846, at which a committee of three was chosen "to appraise the rights of pew holders in the old church of said parish," and Mr. Melvin was a member of this committee. That would seem to indicate residence in town and some interest in the parish at that date.

The drawing of the front elevation of the old Town Hall, later high school, bears the name of Isaac Melvin, architect, and is dated at Cambridge, May 22, 1846. Whether he moved from Lexington to Cambridge between February 16 and May 22, 1846, as we might conjecture, cannot be certified. Besides his work in Lexington, he designed numerous houses and a Baptist church in Cambridge.

He married August 14, 1840, Miss Emma Wright Purkett, born in Boston. He died in California in January, 1852, leaving a widow, but no children. His widow married a Mr. Read and was living in Cambridge, February, 1908, at the age of ninety-five years.

Numerous photographs finished in platinum, the principal measurements * of the church built in 1847, and a floor plan of the church, prepared by William R. Greeley, architect, accompany this paper for illustration, and are preserved in the archives of Lexington Historical Society.

---

* The measurements referred to are as follows:—

MEASUREMENTS, 1908.

First Parish Church, built 1847.

Auditorium:—floor, 67' x 52' 6".
  Screen is 6' from end of auditorium.
  Height of auditorium 27' 10".
  Gallery overhangs auditorium 9' 7" to the frame of window.
  Organ front is 13' 9".
  Square columns on each side of the organ contain the chimneys and are 2' wide.
  Pulpit top is 5' 2" long and 1' 8" wide at ends. Height in front, 4' 10".
  Vestibule from front door to auditorium is 18'. Width, including stairs, 27'.
  Stairs in vestibule leading to gallery have 14 steps 3' 6" wide, 8' 5" risers; treads, [x]" wide.
  Banisters end in a coil at bottom.
  Banister rods are plain rounds 1¼" in diameter.
  Three doors from vestibule to auditorium—centre 4' 6" opening, side doors 3' 5" opening.
  Window sills are 7' long; sash 4' 6" wide.
  End window 11' from corners of church outside of building.
Gallery.
Spire 20' square at base.
  Width of spire at bell room from outsides of window sills is 13' 9".
Bell, 4' in diameter at base; cast in 1872 by Wm. Blake & Co.
Roof rises 9" to every foot level, or at an angle of 37°.

HISTORICAL EVENTS LEADING UP TO THE BATTLES OF LEXINGTON AND CONCORD.

By Alexander Starbuck.   Read December 21, 1909.

The early protests against the Stamp Act, the Boston massacre, the irritation caused by the passage and enforcement of the Boston Port bill, all served to arouse, not only the people of Massachusetts Bay Colony, but their fellow-citizens throughout the country, to a sense of danger which seemed to call for a general consultation as to the method best adapted to meet an impending crisis. Accordingly, at a meeting in Salem in the summer of 1774, an invitation was sent to all the colonies to appoint delegates to meet at Philadelphia on the 5th of September in a general Congress. The invitation was heartily responded to by twelve of the colonies, Georgia alone not being represented. In that Congress were wrought the links that were to bind the colonies together during the struggles of the next decade.*

September 1, 1774, Governor Gage issued a precept to the several towns and districts of the province, commanding the people to choose representatives to the Great and General Court, which he ordered to be convened in Salem, October 5. The reception which this precept encountered

* During the American Revolution there were accredited to the American armies from the several colonies the following numbers of men: New Hampshire, 12,497; Massachusetts, 67,907; Rhode Island, 5,908; Connecticut, 31,939; New York (which probably included Vermont), 17,781; New Jersey, 10,725; Pennsylvania, 25,678; Delaware, 2,386; Maryland, 18,912; Virginia, 26,678; North Carolina, 7,263; South Carolina, 6,417; Georgia, 2,679. From this record it will be seen that New England—exclusive of Vermont—contributed within 268 men of what were sent by all the rest of the country. Massachusetts alone sent more than either the Middle States or the South combined. At that time the population of the Middle States was more than double that of Massachusetts, and the population of the South more than two and a half times that of the Bay Colony. Our people, then, may well feel proud of the record of the Old Bay State in the War for Independence.

in Watertown, Lexington, and Waltham, was a fair sample of its reception throughout the province. Early in September the town of Watertown ordered that its militia should be exercised two hours every week for the three autumn months, and that its stock of arms and ammunition should be inspected. The selectmen of Waltham had voted in July to lay in a stock of ammunition, consisting of four half-barrels of powder, four and one-half hundred weight of bullets, and three hundred flints; and in September the town "Voted and chose Captain William Coolidge, Dea. Elijah Livermore, Capt. Abijah Child and Ensign Abraham Pierce a committee for other towns to send to in any emergency and they to send to other towns on any emergency." This was the local Committee of Correspondence. Lexington as early as 1765 protested against the Stamp Act, and those who offered the stamps for sale did so at their peril. The non-importation resolve was warmly upheld, a Committee of Correspondence was chosen, the duty on tea was roundly denounced, and the town, in response to the action of the town of Boston, returned word, "We trust in God that we shall be ready to sacrifice our estates and everything dear in life, yea, even life itself, in support of the Common Cause." In 1774 Deacon Jonas Stone was chosen a delegate to the Middlesex County Convention which convened in Concord in August, and in November and December of the same year the town voted to provide a suitable number of flints for the soldiers' muskets, to bring up two pieces of cannon from Watertown and mount them, and to provide bayonets for the training of soldiers, and a pair of drums. By the winter of 1774–5 Lexington had a hundred and twenty men enrolled as minute-men.

Nor were Lexington's neighbors lacking in the same patriotic spirit. Woburn, which included Burlington and parts of Winchester and Stoneham, followed the general trend, and her minute-men assisted later at Lexington on the memorable day of the fight. The town of Lincoln on March 15, 1770, voted not to purchase "any article of any person that imports goods contrary to the agreement of the merchants of Boston." Early in 1773 they declared, "We will not be wanting in our assistance according to our ability, in the prosecuting of all such lawful and constitutional measures as shall be thought proper for the continuance of all our rights, privileges and liberties, both civil and religious." November 2, 1773, a Committee of Correspondence was chosen. March 6, 1775, money was appropriated to provide the minute-men with accoutrements. Concord responded patriotically to the address from the people of Boston in 1773, and in 1774 passed strong non-importation resolutions. It was there that the County Convention met in August, 1774, and voted by a hundred and forty-six yeas to four nays: "That it is our opinion these late acts, if quietly submitted to, will annihilate the last vestiges of liberty in this province, and therefore we must be justified by God, and the world, in never submitting to them." Bedford voted in March, 1768, "To concur with the vote of the Town of Boston in October last, to encourage the produce and manufactures of the Province." In March, 1773, the town voted to adopt the agreement of non-intercourse. In March, 1775, an appropriation for the minute-men was voted, and, when the exigency came, twenty-six men marched to the relief of Lexington.*

The action of the people so alarmed Governor Gage

* Deacon Stone, Lexington's representative to the several Provincial Congresses, was one of the committee of three appointed April 27, 1775, to inquire and get an "exact account of the men who were killed, wounded and murdered in the late scene on the 19th inst." He was also one of a committee of three to take the depositions of the survivors and those who had suffered property losses and have them signed and sworn to. June 5 he was appointed one of a committee of two to ascertain what became of an important letter from the South-bridge Indians, and on June 25 he was one of a committee of six to procure 400 spades and shovels for immediate use by the army. July 5 he was one of a committee of eight to procure 200 axes with helves. The damage which Lexington suffered by the raid of the British on April 19 was estimated at £1,761 1s. 15d.

that the Royal Council determined to countermand the summons for the assembly of the Court, and on the 28th of September Governor Gage issued a proclamation setting forth that, in consequence of "the many tumults and disorders" that have taken place since the writs were issued calling for the General Court or Assembly to be convened, "the extraordinary resolves which have been passed in many of the counties, the instructions given by the town of Boston, and some other towns, to their representatives, and the present disordered and unhappy state of the Province, it appears to me highly inexpedient that a Great and General Court should be convened at the time aforesaid; but that a session at some more distant day will best tend to promote His Majesty's service and the good of the Province. I have, therefore, thought fit to declare my intention not to meet the said General Court, at Salem, on the said fifth day of October next. And I do hereby excuse and discharge all such persons as have been, or may be elected and deputed Representatives to serve at the same, from giving their attendance: anything in the aforesaid writs contained to the contrary notwithstanding: whereof all concerned are to take notice and govern themselves accordingly."

Despite the proclamation of the governor, ninety of the representatives elected met at Salem, October 5. The governor not appearing on that day, either in person or by deputy, to administer the usual oaths, the convention formally organized the following day by choosing John Hancock chairman and Benjamin Lincoln clerk. A committee was appointed to consider the governor's proclamation and what measures should be adopted regarding it. The committee reported on the following day by a preamble and four resolutions, which, after setting forth the action already taken by the governor and the court, asserted that under the charter of the province the governor is expressly obliged to convene "upon every last Wednesday in the month of May, every year forever, and at such other times as he shall think fit, and appoint a Great and General Court"; that, having ordered it to be convened on the 5th of October, his conduct in preventing it is contrary to the charter, and unconstitutional; that his power to "adjourn, prorogue and dissolve all Great and General Courts" cannot be operative until they shall have first "met and convened"; that the attempt to supersede and annul the constitutional government by a military force, and his representations that the province is in a tumultuous and disordered state, are reflections the inhabitants have by no means merited; that the pretended cause for the issue of the proclamation of dissolution was in existence when the order for the convening was issued; that some of the causes assigned for this action have "in all good governments been considered among the greatest reasons for convening a parliament or assembly; and, therefore, the proclamation is considered as a further proof, not only of His Excellency's disaffection towards the Province, but of the necessity of its most vigorous and immediate exertions for preserving the freedom and constitution thereof." It was thereupon voted by the members to resolve themselves "into a Provincial Congress, to be joined by such other persons as have been or shall be chosen for that purpose, to take into consideration the dangerous and alarming situation of public affairs in this Province, and to consult and determine on such measures as they shall judge will tend to promote the true interest of His Majesty, and the peace, welfare and prosperity of the Province."

It will be observed that at this time and for a long period subsequently there seems to have been no thought or audible suggestion of independence.

At this Provincial Congress, so important as regards its effect upon the future of the Massachusetts Bay Colony,

Lexington was represented by Deacon Jonas Stone; Watertown, by Captain Jonathan Brown, Mr. John Remington, and Mr. Samuel Fisk; Waltham, by Mr. Jacob Bigelow; and Weston, by Samuel P. Savage, Esq., Captain Braddyl Smith, and Mr. Josiah Smith. At a town meeting in Watertown, October 3, it was voted that "the Collector of Taxes should not pay any more money into the Province treasury at present," and on the 17th of the same month the town voted to mount and equip two pieces of cannon.

October 11 the Congress adjourned to meet in Concord. There it first met in the Old Court House, but, as that room proved too small to accommodate so large an assembly, the sessions were adjourned to the meeting-house. Two sessions were held daily, one at 9 A.M. and the other at 3 P.M. It may be noted here that the adjournment to Concord was carrying out a plan previously determined upon by the several counties, which, long before the issuance of the governor's writs, had chosen delegates to a Provincial Congress to be held in Concord on the second Tuesday of October. At this adjourned Congress John Hancock was chosen president, and Benjamin Lincoln secretary. A committee of fifteen, of which President Hancock was chairman, was appointed "to take into consideration the state of the Province, and report as soon as may be." The committee reported on the following afternoon. The report, which took the form of an address to the governor, said: "The distressed and miserable state of the Province, occasioned by the intolerable grievances and oppressions to which the people are subjected, and the danger and destruction to which they are exposed, of which Your Excellency must be sensible, and the want of a General Assembly, have rendered it indispensably necessary to collect the wisdom of the Province by their delegates in this Congress, to concert some adequate remedy for preventing impending ruin,

and providing for the public safety." The address stated,
further, that the Congress viewed with the utmost concern the hostile preparations "pursued against a people
whose love of order, attachment to Britain, and loyalty
to their prince, have ever been truly exemplary." Earnest
objection was made to the rigorous execution of the Boston
Port Bill, the acts for altering the charter and the administration of justice in the colony, the daily increase in
the number of troops in Boston, and the formidable and
hostile preparations being made on Boston Neck. "Permit us," continued the report, "to ask Your Excellency,
whether an inattentive and unconcerned acquiescence
in such alarming, such menacing measures, would not
evidence a state of insanity; or, whether the delaying to
take every possible precaution for the security of the
Province, would not be the most criminal neglect in a
people heretofore rigidly and justly tenacious of their
constitutional rights?" Especial stress was laid on the
construction of the "fortress" at the entrance of Boston.
His Excellency was assured that "the good people of this
Colony never have had the least intention to do any injury
to His Majesty's troops; but on the contrary, most
earnestly desire that every obstacle to treating them as
fellow-subjects may be immediately removed; but we
are constrained to tell Your Excellency, that the minds
of the people will never be relieved till those hostile works
are demolished; and we request you, as you regard His
Majesty's honor and interest, the dignity and happiness
of the Empire, and the peace and welfare of this Province,
that you immediately desist from the fortress now constructing at the south entrance into the town of Boston,
and restore the pass to its natural state."

This report was adopted with but one dissentient.
History does not record who he was or what were his
reasons for dissenting. It was ordered "that a fair copy

of the foregoing report be taken and presented to His Excellency Thomas Gage Esq., and that a committee be appointed to wait upon him early tomorrow morning with the same." Accordingly, a committee of twenty-one, of which Colonel Jeremiah Lee was chairman, was appointed, and it was also resolved to have the address printed in the Boston newspapers.

At the meeting of the Congress on the afternoon of October 14 the Committee on the State of the Province reported a resolve, which was accepted and ordered printed in the Boston newspapers, advising constables and collectors of taxes, who have or shall have moneys collected on province assessments, not to pay the same or any part thereof to Harrison Gray, Esq., the province treasurer, but "take and observe such orders and directions touching the same, as shall be given them by the several towns and districts by whom they were chosen." Similar advice was given the sheriffs and deputy sheriffs, and the people were recommended to pay assessments "to such person or persons as shall be ordered by the said towns and districts respectively."

On Monday, October 17, Congress met at the meeting-house in Cambridge, and the message was received from Governor Gage, addressed to the committee which had been appointed October 13 to wait upon him. In it he said:—

The previous menaces daily thrown out, and the unusual warlike preparations throughout the country, make it an act of duty in me to pursue the measures I have taken in constructing what you call a fortress, which, unless annoyed, will annoy nobody.

It is surely highly exasperating, as well as ungenerous, even to hint that the lives, liberties or properties of any persons, except avowed enemies, are in danger from Britons; Britain can never harbor the black design of wantonly destroying, or enslaving, any people on earth. And notwithstanding the enmity shewn the king's troops, by withholding from them almost every necessary for their preservation, they have not, as yet, discovered the resentment which might justly be expected to arise from such hostile treatment.

No person can be more solicitous than myself to procure union and harmony between Great Britain and her colonies, and I ardently wish to contribute to the completion of a work so salutary to both countries. But an open and avowed disobedience to all her authority, is only bidding defiance to the mother country, and gives little hopes of bringing a spirited nation to that favorable disposition, which a more decent and dutiful conduct might effect.

Whilst you complain of acts of Parliament that make alterations in your Charter, and put you in some degree on the same footing with many other provinces, you will not forget that by your assembling, you are yourselves subverting that Charter, and now acting in direct violation of your own Constitution.

It is my duty, therefore, however irregular your application is, to warn you of the rock you are upon, and to require you to desist from such illegal and unconstitutional proceedings.

Thomas Gage.

Province House, October 17, 1774.

This message was referred to the same committee that had prepared the address to which it was a reply.

In the next week, committees were appointed "to make as minute an inquiry into the present state and operations of the army" as possible; "to consider what is necessary to be now done for the defence and safety of the Province"; "to report a letter to the selectmen, overseers of the poor, committee of correspondence, and committee of donations, for the town of Boston, desiring their attendance at this Congress, to consult means for the preservation of the town of Boston at this alarming crisis"; and various other topics intimately related to the security of the Massachusetts Bay Colony.

The Committee on the State of the Province reported a series of resolutions, which were in substance as follows: First, that sundry persons, who had accepted commissions under acts of Parliament for changing the form of government and violating the charter of the province, and who shall not give "satisfaction to this injured Province and continent, within ten days of the publication of this resolve, by causing to be published in all the Boston newspapers, acknowledgments of their former misconduct, and renunciations of the commissions and authority mentioned, ought to be considered as infamous betrayers of their country; and that a committee of Congress be ordered to cause their names to be published repeatedly, that the inhabitants of this Province, by having them entered upon the records of each town, as rebels against the State, may send them down to posterity with the infamy they deserve; and that other parts of America may have an opportunity of stigmatizing them in such a way as shall effectually answer a similar purpose." Second, that the good people of the province be recommended "so far to forgive such of the obnoxious persons aforesaid, who shall have given the satisfaction required in the preceding resolve, as not to molest them for their past misconduct."

Committees were appointed who were ordered to carry out the spirit of the resolutions, to report a non-consumption agreement relative to British and India goods, and to report a resolve recommending the total disuse of India teas.

The last-named committee reported in the afternoon of October 21 the following resolution, which was adopted: "That this Congress do earnestly recommend to the people of this Province an abhorrence and detestation of all kinds of East India teas, as the baneful vehicle of a corrupt and venal administration, for the purpose of introducing despotism and slavery into this once happy country; and that every individual in this Province ought totally to disuse the same. And it is also recommended, that every town and district, appoint a committee to post up in some public place the names of all such in their respective towns and districts, who shall sell or consume so extravagant and unnecessary an article of luxury."

On Saturday, October 22, a committee appointed for the purpose reported a resolve recommending that the people of the province observe Thursday, the 15th of December, as a day of thanksgiving because of the "continuance of the gospel among us, and the smiles of Divine Providence upon us with regard to the seasons of the year, and the general health which has been enjoyed; and in particular, from a consideration of the union which so remarkably prevails, not only in this Province, but throughout the continent, at this alarming crisis." It was further enjoined upon the people to humble themselves before God on account of their sins, "for which He hath been pleased, in His righteous judgment, to suffer so great a calamity to befall us as the present controversy between Great Britain and the colonies"; "as also to implore the Divine blessing upon us, that, by the assistance of His grace, we may be enabled to reform whatever is amiss among us; that so God may be pleased to continue to us the blessings we enjoy, and remove the tokens of His displeasure, by causing harmony and union to be restored between Great Britain and these colonies, that we may again rejoice in the smiles of our Sovereign, and in possession of those privileges which have been transmitted to us, and have the hopeful prospect that they shall be handed down entire to posterity under the protestant succession in the illustrious house of Hanover."

Early in the following week the members began to get somewhat restive over the apparent delays of committees to report. On Monday a long debate was had on the report of the Committee appointed to consider what is Necessary to be done for the Defence and Safety of the Province, and the amendments thereto. A committee was appointed "to consider of and report to this Congress the most proper time for this Province to provide a stock of powder, ordnance, and ordnance stores," and the committee was ordered to sit forthwith. The committee appointed to bring in a non-consumption agreement was also ordered to sit forthwith. The Committee on Time to provide Powder, Ordnance, etc., reported that *now* was the proper time, and another committee was at once appointed to determine what number of ordnance and what quantity of ordnance stores and powder would be needed and the expense thereof.

On Tuesday Mr. Wheeler (probably Joseph Wheeler, of Harvard) brought into Congress a letter directed to Dr. Appleton, "purporting," as the record says, "the propriety, that while we are attempting to free ourselves from our present embarrassments, and preserve ourselves from slavery, that we also take into consideration the state and circumstances of the negro slaves in this Province." The letter was read, and a motion was made to have a committee appointed to consider the matter, but it evidently was a somewhat embarrassing subject, and we learn that, "after some debate thereon, the question was put, whether the matter now subside, and it passed in the affirmative." At this session a committee was appointed to inquire into the condition of the stores in the office of the commissary-general.

At the afternoon session of October 25, the Committee on Ordnance and Ordnance Stores reported that it was necessary to procure at once 16 three-pounder field-pieces with their equipments; 4 six-pounder field-pieces; carriages, irons, etc., for 12 battering cannon; 2 eight-inch and 2 thirteen-inch mortars; 20 tons of grape and round shot from 3 to 24 lbs.; 10 tons bomb-shells; 5 tons lead balls; and 1,000 barrels of powder,—at a total expense of £10,737. Also 5,000 arms and bayonets and 75,000 flints at an additional expense of £10,100. The most implicit secrecy was enjoined on the members relative to all these debates in the Congress.

On October 26 the Committee on the Defence and Safety of the Province made its final report, which was considered by paragraphs, amended, and finally accepted "almost unanimously." In substance, the report cited the presence of troops in Boston to execute acts of Parliament subversive of the constitution of the province; the attempt of Governor Gage, with troops, to disperse the inhabitants of Salem while assembled to consider measures for the preservation of their freedom; the fortifying of the capital of the province against the country; the invasion of private property by seizing powder and arms in Boston, provided for the province at the public expense; the endeavor to put the province into a defenceless state; and the entire disregard of the assurances and entreaties of this Congress. And the preamble is followed by a series of eight resolves, which declare for a Committee of Safety, "whose business it shall be, most carefully and diligently to inspect and observe all and every such person or persons as shall, at any time, attempt or enterprise the destruction, invasion, detriment or annoyance of this Province," said committee to have power, "whenever they shall judge it necessary for the safety and defence of the inhabitants of this Province, and their property, against such person or persons as aforesaid, to alarm, muster and cause to be assembled, with the utmost expedition, and completely armed, accoutred, and supplied with provisions sufficient for their support in their march to the place of rendezvous, such and so many of the militia of this Province, as they shall judge necessary for the ends aforesaid and at such place or places as they shall judge proper, and them to discharge as soon as the safety of the Province shall permit." A committee was provided for to look after the reception and support of the militia, and to purchase and provide such arms, accoutrements, etc., as may be needed. Officers were appointed to command the militia when so assembled, and arrangements made to pay officers and men if called into service. Companies of the militia, not already having done so, were recommended to choose and appoint officers, said officers to determine the limits of regiments and to elect field officers to command regiments so formed; the "field officers so elected forthwith to endeavor to enlist one quarter, at the least, of the number of the respective companies, and form them into companies of fifty privates, at the least, who shall equip and hold themselves in readiness, on the shortest notice from the said Committee of Safety to march to the place of rendezvous." Each company was urgently requested to speedily elect its necessary officers. The people were urged immediately to provide themselves with arms and "use their utmost diligence to perfect themselves in military skill." Provision was made for another committee to prepare during the recess of the Congress a plan for regulating and disciplining the militia.

It will be seen by these arrangements that, when the final struggle came, the yeomanry were not such novices as some writers have represented, and why some of them left the half-turned furrow in the field to assemble at the call of an alarm.

On October 27 the Congress chose as a Committee of Safety Hon. John Hancock, Dr. Warren, and Dr. Church for Boston members, and Mr. Devens of Charlestown, Captain White of Brookline, Mr. Palmer of Braintree, Norton Quincy, Esq., of Braintree, Mr. Watson of Cambridge, and Colonel Orne of Marblehead as members from the country. Five commissaries were chosen: Mr. Cheever of Charlestown, Mr. Gill of Princeton, Colonel Lee of Marblehead, Mr. Greenleaf of Newburyport, and Colonel Lincoln of Hingham. Hon. Jedediah Preble was chosen to be first in command of the militia, Hon. Artemas Ward to be second, and Colonel Pomeroy to be third. Henry Gardner, Esq., was subsequently chosen treasurer and receiver-general, and **Mr. Hall of Medford was chosen commissary in place of Mr. Greenleaf, who declined.**

The Committee on non-consumption agreement reported on October 28 the following resolution, which was accepted and ordered published:—

Whereas, the people of this Province have not, as yet, received from the Continental Congress such explicit directions respecting non-importation and non-consumption agreements as are expected; *and whereas*, the greater part of the inhabitants of this colony have lately entered into non-importation and non-consumption agreements, the good effects of which are very conspicuous: Therefore, *Resolved*, That this Congress approve of the said agreements, and earnestly recommend to all the inhabitants of this colony strictly to conform to the same, until the further sense of the Continental or the Provincial Congress is made public. And further, this Congress highly applaud the conduct of those patriotic merchants, who have generously refrained from importing British goods since the commencement of the cruel Boston port bill; at the same time reflect with pain on the conduct of those who have sordidly preferred their private interest to the salvation of their suffering country, by continuing to import as usual; and recommend it to the inhabitants of the Province, that they discourage the conduct of said importers by refusing to purchase any articles whatever of them.

At the same session it was "Ordered, That Capt. Heath, Doct. Warren and Doct. Church be a committee to take care of, and lodge in some safe place in the country, the warlike stores now in the Commissary General's office, and that the matter be conducted with the greatest secrecy." It was also "*Resolved*, That the Committee of Correspondence of the town of Worcester be desired to take proper care that the bayonets, the property of this Province, now in the hands of Col. Chandler, be removed to some safe place at a distance from his house."

On October 29 the committee appointed to consider what military exercise it was advisable for the people of the province to adopt reported, and the following resolve was accepted and ordered published in the Boston newspapers: "That it be recommended to the inhabitants of this Province, that in order to their perfecting themselves in the military art, they proceed in the method ordered by His Majesty in the year 1764, it being, in the opinion of this Congress, best calculated for appearance and defence."

On the same day the Congress unanimously accepted a reply to the governor's letter, and appointed a committee to wait upon him with it. The address expressed astonishment that no heed had been paid to the earnest protestations of the delegates in Congress. It continued: "We are surprised at your saying, that 'what we call a fortress, unless annoyed, will annoy nobody,' when, from your acquaintance with the Constitution of Britain, and of the Province over which you have been by His Majesty commissioned to preside, you must know, that barely keeping a standing army in the Province in time of peace, without consent of the representatives is against law, and must be considered as a great grievance to the subject, a grievance which this people could not, with a due regard to their freedom, endure, was there not reason to hope that His Majesty, upon being undeceived, would order redress." "Have not," continues the letter, "invasions of private property, by Your Excellency, been repeatedly made in Boston? Have not the inhabitants of Salem, whilst peaceably assembled for concerting measures to preserve their freedom, and unprepared to defend themselves, been in imminent danger from your troops? Have you not, by removing the ammunition of the Province, and by all other means in your power, endeavored to put it in a state utterly defenceless? Have you not expressly declared that 'resentment might justly be expected' from your troops, merely in consequence of a refusal of some inhabitants of the Province to supply them with property undeniably their own? Surely these are questions founded on incontestable facts, which, we think, must prove that while the 'avowed enemies' of Great Britain and the colonies, are protected by Your Excellency, the lives, liberties, and properties of the inhabitants of the Province, who are real friends to the British Constitution, are greatly endangered, whilst under the control of your standing army. It must be a matter of grief to every true Briton, that the honor of the British troops is sullied by the infamous errand on which they are sent to America; and whilst, in the unjust cause on which you are engaged, menaces will never produce submission from the people of this Province, Your Excellency, as well as the army, can only preserve your honor by refusing to submit to the most disgraceful prostitution of subserving plans so injurious, and so notoriously iniquitous and cruel to this people." It concludes thus: "And although we are willing to put the most favorable construction on the warning you have been pleased to give us of the 'rock on which we are,' we beg leave to inform you that our constituents do not expect, that, in the execution of that important trust which they have reposed in us, we should be wholly guided by your advice. We trust, sir, that we shall not fail in our duty to our country and loyalty to our King, or in a proper respect to Your Excellency." This reply it was ordered to have published in the newspapers. It was also voted to publish a synopsis of the acts of the Congress of public interest. John Pigeon of Newton and Captain William Heath of Roxbury were added to the Committee of Safety, and the Congress adjourned to meet again November 23 at Cambridge, which was also decided to be the most eligible place for the meetings of the Committee of Safety.

November 23 Congress again met. Various matters, foreshadowing impending legislation, occupied the most of the time during the first week. A committee of five was appointed to make as just an estimate as may be of the loss and damage of every kind "accrued to the Province by the operation of the Boston Port bill and the act for altering the civil government, from their commencement to this time." Another committee was appointed to take into consideration the state of manufactures in the province and see how they may be improved; another, "to devise some means of keeping up a correspondence between this Province, Montreal and Quebec, and of gaining very frequent intelligence from thence of their movements"; another, "to state the amount of the sums which have been extorted from us since the year 1763,* by the operation of certain acts of the British Parliament." John Hancock, Thomas Cushing, Samuel Adams, John Adams, and Robert Treat Paine were chosen delegates to the American Congress to be held at Philadelphia on or before the 10th of May next.

December 5 the report of the committee appointed to take into consideration the state of rights, state of grievances, and the association, as stated by the Continental Congress, was made. The proceedings of the Continental Congress were warmly approved. To quote from the report, "the American bill of rights therein contained, appears to be formed with the greatest ability and judgment; to be founded on the immutable laws of nature and reason, the principles of the English Constitution, and the respective charters and constitutions of the Colonies; and to be worthy of their most vigorous support, as essentially necessary to liberty; likewise the ruinous and iniquitous measures, which, in violation of their rights, at present convulse and threaten destruction to America,

* The year when the Treaty of Paris closed the French and Indian War.

appear to be clearly pointed out, and judicious plans adopted for defeating them." Resolutions were passed thanking the members of the Continental Congress for their excellent service, denouncing the merchants who continued to import interdicted goods, and favoring even more strenuous measures against their purchase by the people of the province whose sympathies were with the struggling colonists; recommending the immediate choice of committees of inspection to see that such measures were made effectual, and directing the publication in all the newspapers of the province of this report of the committee, as well as the sending of copies of it to all the towns and districts in the province.

December 6 a committee was appointed to correspond with the people of Canada, and another committee, which had been appointed to prepare an appeal for donations to aid the people of Boston and Charlestown who were suffering from the effects of the Boston Port Bill, made its report. It contained, among other provisions, a special appeal to the clergymen to bring this exigency to the attention of their parishioners. The names of the fifteen recalcitrant councillors who were serving under the mandamus of the governor, and had not shown any disposition to renounce their commissions and espouse the cause of the people, were read and ordered "published repeatedly."

On the 7th of December it was resolved that a committee be appointed, "consisting of one gentleman from each county, and one from each maritime town of this colony, to prepare from the best authentic evidence which can be procured, a true state of the number of the inhabitants, and of the quantities of exports and imports of goods, wares, and merchandize, and of the manufactures of all kinds, within the colony to be used by our delegates at the Continental Congress, to be held at Philadelphia, on or about the tenth of May next."

On the following day the report of the Committee on the State of Manufactures of the Province was read, amended, and as amended was accepted. The report recommended to the people the improvement of the breed of sheep and the greatest possible increase in the same, as well as the preferable use of our own woollen manufactures. It was recommended to manufacturers that they ask only reasonable prices for their goods, and especially that they make a very careful sorting of wool, so that it might be manufactured to the greatest advantage, and as much as possible into the best goods. The raising of hemp and flax was recommended, and the manufacture of the flax-seed into oil. The making of nails, steel, tin plate, fire-arms, gunlocks and other locks, saltpetre, gunpowder, glass, buttons, salt, and wool-combers' combs, was strongly advised. As several paper mills were now usefully employed, it was advised that there be a careful saving and collecting of rags, and that manufacturers pay a generous price for them. The encouragement of horn-smiths was recommended, as well as the preferable use of stockings and other hosiery woven among ourselves. The raising and curing of madder was desired. The argument leading up to the recommendations is particularly interesting. It reads: "As the happiness of particular families arises in a great degree from their being more or less dependent upon others, and as the less occasion they have for any article belonging to others, the more independent, and consequently the happier they are,—so the happiness of every political body of men upon earth is to be estimated, in a great measure, upon their greater or less dependence upon any other political bodies; and from hence arises a forcible argument, why every state ought to regulate their internal policy in such a manner as to furnish themselves, within their own body, with every necessary article for subsistence and defence, otherwise their political existence will depend upon others who may take advantage of such weakness and reduce them to the lowest state of vassalage and slavery." We may well believe that the writers of that report were strong protectionists, and that they were warmly supported by the Congress to which they were delegates. The committee further recommended, in order to carry out more effectually the several resolutions, that "a society or societies be established for the purposes of introducing and establishing such arts and manufactures as may be useful to this people, and are not yet introduced, and the more effectually establishing such as we already have among us." It was recommended, in conclusion, to the inhabitants of the province "to make use of our own manufactures, and those of our sister colonies, in preference to all other manufactures." On the same day two general officers were elected by the Congress, Colonel John Thomas and Colonel William Heath.

The First Provincial Congress adjourned on the 10th of December, prior to which the orders and resolves relating to returning moneys for taxes to the provincial treasurer rather than to the king's officers and those pertaining to manufactures and the purchase of imported goods were reaffirmed, and an address "To the Freeholders and other Inhabitants of the Towns and Districts of Massachusetts Bay" was accepted and ordered distributed through the province. The address put in strong language the arguments urging the people to resist the invasion of their constitutional rights, and concluded in these words:—

With the utmost cheerfulness we assure you of our determination to stand or fall with the liberties of America; and while we humbly implore the Sovereign Disposer of all things, to whose divine providence the rights of His creatures cannot be indifferent, to correct the errors, and alter the measures of an infatuated ministry, we cannot doubt of His support even in the extreme difficulties which we all may have to encounter.   May all means devised by the General Congress of America, and assemblies or conventions of the colonies, be resolutely executed, and happily succeeded; and may this injured people be reinstated in the full exercise of their rights without the evils and devastations of a civil war.

The Royalists at this time were not without organization.   Timothy Ruggles, one of the complained-of councillors, prepared and sent to the town of Hardwick, where he formerly resided, articles of association in which the adherents of the Crown agreed:—

(1) That we will, on all occasions, with our lives and fortunes, stand by and assist each other in the defence of life, liberty and property, whenever the same shall be attacked or endangered by any bodies of men, riotously assembled, upon any pretence or under any authority not warranted by the laws of the land.   (2) That we will, upon all occasions, mutually support each other in the free exercise and enjoyment of our undoubted right to liberty, in eating, drinking, buying, selling, communing and acting, what, with whom, and as we please, consistent with the laws of God and of the King.   (3) That we will not acknowledge, or submit to the pretended authority of any Congresses, committees of correspondence, or other unconstitutional assemblies of men; but will, at the risk of our lives, if need be, oppose the forcible exercise of all such authority.   (4) That we will, to the utmost of our power, promote, encourage, and, when called to it, enforce obedience to the rightful authority of our most gracious sovereign, King George the Third, and of his laws.   (5) That when the person or property of any one shall be invaded or threatened by any committees, mobs, or unlawful assemblies, the others of us, will, upon notice received, forthwith repair, properly armed, to the person whom, or place where such invasion or threatening shall be, and will, to the utmost of our power, defend such person and his property, and, if need be, will oppose and repel force with force.   (6) That if any one of us shall unjustly and unlawfully be injured in his person or property, by any such assemblies as before mentioned, the others of us will, unitedly, demand, and, if in our power, compel the offenders, if known, to make full reparation and satisfaction for such

injury; and if all other means of security fail we will have recourse to the natural law of retaliation.

Fortunately for the Royalists, their bark was much worse than their bite.

Before considering the work of the Second Provincial Congress, a brief review may well be taken of the situation in England. There the opposition encountered in the colonies, especially in that of the Massachusetts Bay, excited a storm of indignation with the governing ministry. A bill was introduced into Parliament early in February, restricting the commerce of New England to Great Britain, Ireland, and the British West Indies, and prohibiting the colonies from carrying on any fishery on the Banks of Newfoundland or any other part of the North American coast. Thus the fisheries, which the people of New England, unaided and at their own expense, had wrested from France, were closed against them. The whale fishery was hard hit also, and it was on this phase of the bill that Edmund Burke made his ever memorable speech, in which he said:—

For some time past, Mr. Speaker, has the Old World been fed from the New. The scarcity which you have felt would have been a desolating famine, if this child of your old age,—if America, with a true filial piety, with a Roman charity, had not put the full breast of its youthful exuberance to the mouth of its exhausted parent. Turning from the agricultural resources of the Colonies, consider the wealth which they have drawn from the sea by their fisheries. The spirit in which that interesting employment has been exercised ought to raise your esteem and admiration. Pray, Sir, what in the world is equal to it? Pass by the other parts, and look at the manner in which the People of New England have of late carried on the whale fishery. Whilst we follow them among the tumbling mountains of ice, and behold them penetrating into the deepest frozen recesses of Hudson's Bay and Davis' Straits, whilst we are looking for them beneath the Arctic Circle, we hear that they have pierced into the opposite region of Polar cold, that they are at the antipodes, and engaged under the frozen Serpent of the South. Falkland Island, which seemed too remote and romantic an object for the grasp of national ambition, is but a stage and resting-place in the progress of their victorious industry. Nor is the equinoctial heat more discouraging to them than the accumulated winter of both the Poles. We know that whilst some of them draw the line and strike the harpoon on the coast of Africa, others run the longitude, and pursue their gigantic game, along the coast of Brazil. No sea but what is vexed by their fisheries. No climate that is not a witness to their toils. Neither the perseverance of Holland, nor the activity of France, nor the dexterous and firm sagacity of English enterprise, ever carried this most perilous mode of hardy industry to the extent to which it has been pushed by this recent People; a People who are still, as it were, but in the gristle, and not yet hardened into the bone, of manhood. When I contemplate these things,—when I know that the Colonies in general owe little or nothing to any care of ours, and that they are not squeezed into this happy form by the constraints of a watchful and suspicious Government, but that, through a wise and salutary neglect, a generous nature has been suffered to take her own way to perfection,— when I reflect upon these effects, when I see how profitable they have been to us, I feel all the pride of power sink, and all presumption in the wisdom of human contrivances melt, and die away within me. My rigor relents, I pardon something to the spirit of liberty.

But eloquence and logic alike were wasted. The bill became a law, and the colonies and England drifted further apart.

The Second Provincial Congress did not assemble until February 1, 1775, when it met at Cambridge. In the meantime the several towns in the province had been by no means inactive. In Waltham the inhabitants in town-meeting assembled, January 9, 1775, put on record the following: "The question was then put to know the minds of the town, whether they will all be prepared and stand ready equipt as minute men; and it passed in the affirmative." There could have been but few, if any, dissen-

tients, for no division of the vote is recorded. In Watertown, January 2, it was voted in town-meeting "that a
minute company should be formed for military exercises,
each man being allowed for his attendance once a week
four coppers." Captain Samuel Barnard was in command
of this company, and John Stratton and Phineas Stearns
the first and second lieutenants, respectively. The action
taken by Waltham and Watertown was only an example
of what was done throughout the province.

The Committees of Safety and Supplies were busy, too,
procuring and caring for arms, ammunition, accoutrements, commissary supplies, etc. At a meeting of the
committees at the house of Mrs. Whittemore in Charlestown, January 5, 1775, among other important votes
passed relating to supplies was one "that the battering
cannon carriages be carried to the cannon at Waltham,
and that the cannon and carriages remain there until
further orders."

At the Second Congress Captain Jonathan Brown represented Watertown, Colonel Braddyl Smith represented
Weston, and Jonas Dix, Esq., represented Waltham.
Hon. John Hancock was again chosen president, and
Benjamin Lincoln secretary. A committee of nineteen
to take into consideration the state and circumstances of
the province, was selected.

February 4 the secretary was directed to write to Colonel
Roberson [Robinson], desiring him to deliver the four brass
field pieces and the two brass mortars now in his hands, the
property of the province, to the order of the Committee
of Safety. On the 13th of February the committee voted
that Captain White and Colonel Lincoln be a committee
to receive the four brass field pieces, and the brass
mortars, now in Colonel Robinson's hands, the property
of the province, "and as soon as may be, remove them
to the town of Concord, and they are to inform him that

the committee agree, in case of a rupture with the troops, that the said field pieces shall be for the use of the artillery companies in Boston and Dorchester, and if matters are settled without, said field pieces are to be returned to said Robinson."

It was reported by the Committee of Correspondence of Boston and others that certain persons were supplying the king's troops, then in Boston, with iron for wagons, canvas, tent poles, etc., to enable them to take the field against the colonists. A committee having this matter referred to them reported on February 7 resolutions that,

should any person or persons presume to supply the troops now stationed at Boston or elsewhere in said Province, with timber, boards, spars, pickets, tent-poles, canvas, bricks, iron, wagons, carts, carriages, entrenching tools, or any materials for making any of the carriages or implements aforesaid; with horses or oxen for draught; or any other materials whatever, which may enable them to annoy, or in any manner distress said inhabitants, he or they so offending shall be held in the highest detestation, and deemed inveterate enemies to America, and ought to be prevented and opposed by all reasonable means whatever.

It was deemed probable that large quantities of straw might be needed in case the people were obliged to resort to arms, and persons having straw were desired not to sell or dispose of it excepting to the people of the province for private use or for the use of the province. These resolves were ordered published in the newspapers of the province.

On the afternoon of that day (February 7) it is recorded, "In consideration of the coldness of the season, and that the Congress sit in a house without fire, *Resolved*, That all those members who incline thereto may sit with their hats on while in Congress."

The following day a petition was received from Boice and Clark, praying that Congress take steps to encourage the collection of linen rags in their respective towns, which later was done. Messrs. Boice and Clark owned a paper mill at Milton, and it is not improbable that the former was John Boice, who afterwards established a paper mill on the banks of the Charles River in Waltham.

On February 9 a special committee appointed to prepare an address to the people of the Massachusetts Bay Colony presented a report which was accepted and ordered printed. The address set forth the grievances of the colonists, and earnestly urged continued preparations for resistance. It said,—

Though we deprecate a rupture with the mother state, yet we must still urge you to every preparation for your necessary defence; for, unless you exhibit to your enemies such a firmness as shall convince them that you are worthy of that freedom your ancestors fled here to enjoy, you have nothing to expect but the vilest and most abject slavery.

The address closed with the hope that

you will still continue steadfast, and having regard to the dignity of your characters as freemen, and those generous sentiments resulting from your natural and political connections, you will never submit your necks to the galling yoke of despotism prepared for you; but with a proper sense of your dependence on God, nobly defend those rights which Heaven gave, and no man ought to take from us.

On the 11th of February it was determined that the Committee of Safety should appoint one of their number commissary to deliver stores, ordnance, arms, etc., as directed by the committee, until the constitutional army shall take the field. It was also resolved that the committee should take charge of a lot of bayonets and other implements purchased for the province.

On the 13th of February arrangements were made to obtain information respecting the arms and equipment in each town in the province and the number of minute-men who were enrolled, also to spread throughout the colony plain and simple directions for making saltpetre.

It is quite evident that the delegates in the Congress believed there was continual danger of a *coup d'état*, and were determined not to be caught unawares, for on the 15th of February Congress resolved,—

That the great law of self-preservation, calls upon the inhabitants of this Colony, immediately to prepare against every attempt that may be made to attack them by surprise; and it is, upon serious deliberation, most earnestly recommended to the militia in general, as well as the detached part of it in minute-men, that they spare neither time, pains nor expense, at so critical a juncture, in perfecting themselves forthwith in military discipline, and that skilful instructors be provided for those companies which may not already be provided therewith; and it is recommended to the towns and districts in this Colony, that they encourage such persons as are skilled in the manufacturing of firearms and bayonets, diligently to apply themselves thereto, for supplying such of the inhabitants as may still be deficient.

It was further voted that

as an encouragement to American manufacturers of firearms and bayonets that Congress will give preference to, and purchase from them, so many effective arms and bayonets as can be delivered in a reasonable time, upon notice given to this Congress at its next session.

At the session of February 16 it was voted that Thursday, March 16, should be observed as a day of fasting and prayer,

to humble ourselves before God, on account of our sins; to implore His forgiveness; to beg His blessing upon the labors of the field, upon our merchandize, fishery and manufactures, and upon the various means used to recover and preserve our just rights and liberties; and also, that His blessing may rest upon all the British empire, upon George the Third, our rightful King, and upon all the royal family, that they may all be great and lasting blessings to the world; to implore the outpourings of His spirit, to enable us to bear and suffer whatever His holy and righteous Providence may see fit to lay upon us; and also humbly to supplicate His direction and assistance, to discover and reform whatever is amiss, so that He may be pleased to remove these heavy afflictions, those tokens of His displeasure, and may cause harmony and union to be restored between Great Britain and these colonies, and that we may again rejoice in the free and undisturbed exercise of all those rights and privileges, for the enjoyment of which, our pious and virtuous ancestors braved every danger, and transmitted the fair possession down to their children, to be by them handed down entire to the latest posterity.

On February 16 Congress adjourned to meet in Concord March 22. At its session on April 1 it adopted an address to the Indians of Stockbridge and other localities who had enlisted as minute-men, expressing its pleasure and satisfaction at their action. On April 5 Congress prescribed forms of oaths for the use of the army and a series of fifty-two Articles for its government.

On March 9 one Thomas Ditson, Jr., of Billerica, an adherent of the colonists, was assaulted, tarred, and feathered, and carried through the streets of that town by a party of British soldiers, attended by some officers. The assault appeared to be entirely unprovoked and done in a spirit of malice; and on April 7 Congress took official notice of it by a letter to the selectmen of Billerica, expressing its indignation. Naturally, these petty acts of English soldiers, which were allowed to pass unrebuked by their officers, did not tend to promote good feeling on the part of the people; and every day witnessed a more marked separation between the governor and his troops, on the one hand, and the inhabitants of the colony, on the other.

On March 9, also, Congress prepared and had sent to the Committees of Correspondence of several towns a letter admonishing them to put the militia and minute-men in the best posture for defence whenever any exigency might require their aid, to act, however, only on the defensive, until the further order of Congress. At the same time a letter was sent to the colonies of Connecticut, Rhode Island, and New Hampshire, notifying them of the alarming conditions confronting the people of Massachusetts Bay.

On the 12th of April Congress chose County Committees of Correspondence of five each, to whom the town and district committees were to report. Captain Jonathan Brown of Watertown was one of those selected for Middlesex County.

We are now come to the time of the expedition of the British troops to Lexington and Concord.

It will be seen, therefore, by the records of the Provincial Congresses and of the several towns that the people of Massachusetts were by no means in a state of entire unpreparedness when hostilities actually commenced. The experiences of previous wars, of which the colonists had had a surfeit, had made many of them familiar with the duties of the soldier; and military titles, acquired in actual service, were by no means rare. Add to these experiences the fact, as shown by the records, that our people were thoroughly aroused to the emergency, kept in constant training for several months before the actual breaking out of hostilities, and that they held themselves as minute-men, ready equipped and in instant readiness for any call, and we can readily see that the rapid gathering of men at Lexington and Concord prepared to oppose the advance and harass the retreat of the British troops was not the random gathering of undisciplined mobs, but rather the working out by trained men of a matured plan.

The Committee of Safety on the day following the memorable struggles at Lexington and Concord sent the following circular to the several towns:—

Gentlemen:—The barbarous murders committed upon our innocent brethren, on Wednesday, the 19th instant, have made it absolutely necessary, that we immediately raise an army to defend our wives and children from the butchering hands of an inhuman soldiery, who incensed at the obstacles they meet with in their bloody progress, and enraged at being repulsed from the field of slaughter, will, without the least doubt, take the first opportunity in their power, to ravage this devoted country with fire and sword. We conjure you, therefore, by all that is sacred, that you give assistance in forming an army. Our all is at stake. Death and devastation are the certain consequences of delay. Every moment is infinitely precious. An hour lost may deluge your country in blood, and entail perpetual slavery upon the few of our posterity who may survive the carnage. We beg and entreat, as you will answer to your country, to your own consciences, and above all, as you will answer to *God* himself, that you will hasten and encourage by all possible means, the enlistment of men to form the army, and send them forward to headquarters at Cambridge, with that expedition, which the vast importance and instant urgency of the affair demand.

SOME MEMORIES OF THE BAPTIST CHURCH IN LEXINGTON.*

By Mrs. Alice D. Goodwin. October 4, 1909.

In compliance with the request of Rev. Mr. Knowles I have jotted down a few reminiscences of my early association with the Baptist church.

I fear they will be of little interest at the present time, since they are brought forth from the dim recesses of a shadowy past, peopled mostly by those who long ago finished their earthly career.

My parents, Captain William D. Phelps and his wife, were active and honored members of the church from the year 1838 until their death, serving its interests faithfully through many experiences of weakness and discouraging hindrances to its growth.

They were intimate friends of the first-settled pastor, Rev. Oliver Augustus Dodge, and of his wife, for whom I was named. After the early death of her lamented husband, Mrs. Dodge removed to Haverhill, Mass. Her two daughters, Alice and Mary Frances, were graduates of Bradford Academy in the neighboring village. Both of them died in early young womanhood. Their mother spent the remainder of her life with relatives in New Hampshire. For many years the whole family have slept their last sleep in our village cemetery.

My first recollections of the church are of a large audience-room, with a row of six pews on each side of the

* Though this paper and the one following were not read before the Lexington Historical Society, it is thought proper to preserve them in this volume because of events which they record in connection with the growth of one of the religious organizations in the town. The Baptist society here was started in 1834, and the seventy-fifth anniversary of the beginning was observed by interesting exercises held in the church, October 4, 1909. The two papers referred to were prepared for and read on that occasion.

high pulpit, whose occupants could see and be seen by their fellow-worshippers, and with a double row of pews extending through the centre, separated from the wall pews by two side aisles. A large stove in the rear, under the choir loft, did its best, but unsuccessfully, to create a comfortable temperature during the winter months. The singing seats in the rear were approached by stairs on either side of the vestibule. They contained several tiers of high-backed seats rising one above the other and surmounted by a broad platform, upon which stood the reed organ facing the choir. From this high perch the organist at *her* end could look down and across at the minister who occupied the pulpit at *his* end of the church. There were three large windows on each side of the building, three at one end and two at the other. These windows, with two exceptions, contained seventy-two panes of glass apiece, and I derived much entertainment from counting them during the Sunday services, which were more edifying to the parents in the congregation than to their small children. Eleven windows with their many panes formed quite an exercise in multiplication for my youthful brain, and my interest in this arithmetical process continued unabated from Sunday to Sunday, for a long time. Such big, bare windows and such a barnlike interior were not calculated to foster the æsthetic tastes of the rising generation! The low-studded vestry in the basement was furnished with rows of wooden benches on its bare floor, and was dark and dismal enough for the prison of another Bonnivard.

It was here that the Sunday-school sessions were held, conducted by earnest, faithful teachers, who, with few reference or text books at their command, perhaps did as good work as their successors. We were taught to commit many portions of Scripture to memory,—a very important feature, it seems to me, in all Sunday-school training. The Ten Commandments, portions of the Psalms, the Beatitudes, and whole chapters of the New Testament were as familiar to us as the alphabet. To this day these selections from the Bible are fraught with fragrant memories of good Mrs. Tidd and others who were my early teachers.

The meagre contents of the Sunday-school library consisted largely of memoirs of pious children and biographies of worthy men, which were considered profitable and stimulating for their young readers. If I have been moderately truthful through life, it may be because I read over and over the tales of Amelia Opie upon white lies and their serious consequences. This library book was greatly prized by my excellent mother because of its valuable lessons for her children.

I will add that children attended church and Sunday-school at an early age when I was young, without regard to their wishes in the matter. If my sister and I remained at home for any reason, we were required to learn and recite to our parents either five long or ten short Bible verses. Very carefully did we pore over the sacred pages to count the lines and find the smallest number for our purpose.

The singing-books for our use in Sunday-school were the size of a small primer, and contained such selections as "Hail to the brightness of Zion's glad morning" and "A poor wayfaring man of grief." We were led and taught by Deacon Albert Fessenden, who was also an important factor in the church choir. For many years the choir had a violin, 'cello, and bass viol for accompaniments to the voices.

By the time a reed organ was introduced into the choir I was old enough to be installed as the first organist. Having already taken some piano lessons, I was sent into Boston for instruction in thorough-bass, and for six years, until I went away to a boarding-school, I hardly missed a Sunday from my post of duty. With the assistance of two young friends of the opposite sex, who vied with one another in serving as blowers, I played the good old tunes of "Hebron," "Ware," "Balerma," "Olmutz," "Antwerp," "Rock of Ages," and many others from the Carmina Sacra, for a choir of varied talents and dimensions. In those days Rev. Ira Leland was the pastor, and he never failed to hand me his selected list of hymns for morning and afternoon, in season for the early morning rehearsals. A mildly insane man named Robinson, who lived at the town poorhouse, had the habit for quite a while of attending these rehearsals, taking his place at my side and watching my fingers with a pleased smile of admiration as they manipulated the keys. Finally, my father invited him to take a seat in the minister's pew, and this attention was so pleasing to him that he ceased visiting the choir.

In Mr. Leland's congregation were a number of families whose names are almost or quite unknown to the present generation. There was Mr. Eliab Brown, whose coming was heralded by a very squeaky pair of boots as he wended his way to a pew well up in front, followed by his meek wife. He had no children of his own and no liking for those belonging to his neighbors. They consequently disliked him in return, and lost no opportunity to play tricks upon "old Uncle 'Liab," as they called him. Tall Mrs. Winning, owner of the "Winning Farm" in "Scotland," with a pewful of tall sons and daughters, occupied a side pew. A numerous family of Bosworths, also from "Scotland," had a pew behind them, while in front sat Deacon Locke, his wife, and daughter Elizabeth, now Mrs. Fisher. Mrs. Tidd was a constant attendant, and her husband, who was a Unitarian, always escorted her to the church door, and called for her with his chaise after the service was ended at the Unitarian church. He was noted for his politeness, and this was certainly a pleasant way of showing it, as well as a good example for other husbands.

Time fails me for mentioning details concerning the Hosmers, Chadbournes, Norcrosses, Munroes, Trasks, Fiskes, Fessendens, Fillebrowns, and other interesting families.

Mr. George C. Goodwin, my husband's father, came to Lexington in 1848, and during his residence here of over ten years was active in the church and all its meetings. He filled the position of Sunday-school superintendent in Lexington and Charlestown for more than a quarter of a century.

Among the summer residents in town who attended the Baptist church were the Blakes, Sawyers, and Whitmores. The last-named family owned the Brown estate on Hancock Street. They were very constant in attending the Sunday services. Their substantial carriage with its span of gray horses deposited a portion of the family at the church door, the others following on foot. Mr. and Mrs. Whitmore, five daughters, and two sons, filled two pews, and were a most welcome addition to our numbers. One of the daughters is now a countess, and has resided in France for many years. Two others have made their home at the Russell House for several winters.

Others will doubtless make mention this evening of further events in the pastorates of Mr. Leland and his successors, and I will therefore bring to a close these random recollections with my heartfelt congratulations upon the church's present prosperity and its honored place in our community, so unlike its early standing when it was small and feeble and its members were looked down upon by those belonging to the more prosperous denominations, while the few children belonging to the parish were taunted by their schoolmates as being "little Baptists,"—a term of derision which sank very deeply in our young hearts.

It is good to feel that the years have brought about friendly relations between our various churches, that we are constantly gaining in charity, love, and neighborly regard for one another, and that we can agree with the one who says,

> "So many Gods, so many creeds,
>   So many paths, that wind and wind,
>   When just the art of being *kind*
> Is all this sad world needs."

For kindness is the fruit of love, and love is the greatest of all things in this world of ours.

GROWTH OF THE BAPTIST CHURCH.*

BY MRS. ESTHER TIDD BARRETT. OCTOBER 4, 1909.

During Dr. Pryor's pastorate the ladies of his church and congregation formed a sewing circle, which held its meetings at the homes of the members. The average attendance was seventeen. So productive were the efforts of these workers that they considered the plan of holding a fair to dispose of their work. When kind-hearted neighbors knew of this plan, they said, "The Baptists have never had anything of this kind, and, if they do have a fair, we will make it a success." The fair was held June 21, 1875, and netted for the sewing circle $400. The circle voted to use part of this sum to pay the debt that had hung over the church through several years; the rest was to be put in the bank to be used for repairing the house of worship. There were about two hundred dollars of the money put in the bank.

After Dr. Pryor resigned, the church appointed a committee on pulpit supply. By seeming accident the committee were led to ask Colonel Conwell, then widely known as a lawyer and a lecturer, to supply the pulpit for one Sunday. He did so, and came repeatedly, with the result that he relinquished the practice of law and was ordained to the ministry, and at once entered upon the work as pastor.

At this time, responding to earnest solicitation, Mr. and Mrs. Quincy Chandler and Mr. and Mrs. A. M. Tucker gave us their services as choir; and this quartette continued their generosity through several months. They became a very powerful factor in promoting the prosperity of the church.

Repairs on the church building were begun almost

* See footnote, page 158.

immediately. Colonel Conwell took a shovel and began to dig. A townsman, passing by, handed him $100 with which to hire some one else to dig. The gift was very gladly accepted, but our pastor continued his digging.

The services were enjoyed by very large congregations, and it was not an unusual thing to find seventy or eighty dollars as the result of the morning and evening collections of a single Sunday. This was a most welcome replenishing of the treasury of the church, which at the coming of Colonel Conwell contained only $1.50.

All the people of the church and congregation worked with enthusiastic energy and determination. While the church had been few in number, the members, without exception, had given to the extent of very great self-denial; and now they continued to do so, and they were gladdened by the generosity of many of the more opulent townspeople. With unremitting earnestness the work went on. Many new members were added to the church,—some by letter, but more by baptism; and in every way the church received rich blessing.

More money was needed. A committee of two hundred were asked to unite in getting up a fair. Exactly how many served on this committee it is impossible to ascertain; but the workers were many and energetic, and as a result a fair was held in the Town Hall, lasting four successive days and evenings. Checks came in from many friends out of town, and this fair netted from all sources $1,600.

The kindness of the great number who had no connection with the Baptist church was wonderful. The Catholics, by advice of their priest, came in large numbers to the fair, and were generous in their expenditures. Thus went on and prospered the great work of rebuilding the house of worship and of adding to the church many new members. During eighteen months over eight thousand dollars had been raised.

OBITUARIES.

HANNAH MCLEAN GREELEY.

1848–1906.

Hannah Bishop McLean, daughter of Dudley Bester McLean and Mary Payne, and the oldest of their five children, was born in Simsbury, Conn., January 17, 1848, and died in Lexington, Mass., February 2, 1906. Her mother and sister, two of the three brothers, and her own two sons and daughter survived her. The McLeans, estimated by their worldly goods, were poor; but as New Englanders of the old native stock they were surpassingly wealthy in all the elements of a sound and vigorous character.

With such a parentage, and growing up amidst the toils and discipline of a simple farm life, Hannah's early experiences made a training school of a kind that was well calculated to develop in her the qualities of industry and self-reliance, and an abiding sense of the happiness which comes from sacrificing self in service for others. At the age of seven she helped her mother sew and cook and take care of the younger children. Rocking Georgie * in the old wooden cradle with her foot and knitting with her hands, she would read to the others from a volume of Dickens, kept open on her lap by a clasp. Such scenes as these suggest what her daily occupations were throughout childhood. After a few years in the "deestrict" school, she graduated at twelve to the position of assistant to the old Calvinist minister of the town,—her grandfather, Allan McLean. He was physically blind, and

* George Payne McLean, Governor of Connecticut in 1901–2; now (1911) United States senator from that State.

little Hannah had to write from dictation his sermons, copy manuscripts, lead him about on his parish calls, and guide him to and from the meeting-house on Sundays.

Considerations of economy forced her at the age of fourteen to become a teacher in the local school. Her salary the first year was twenty-four dollars, of which she kept only half for her own uses. Naturally strong intellectual interests inspired in her a determination to acquire a higher education; and without other than self-aids she fitted herself for admission to Mt. Holyoke. After working her way through that seminary, graduating with honor, she had a varied experience as a teacher, first in Bishop Whipple's school at Faribault, Minn., afterwards in an institution at St. John's, Newfoundland, and finally in the Prospect Hill School for Girls at Greenfield, Mass. During these few years of school-teaching her weekly letters to her mother show a devoted and often homesick daughter looking anxiously forward to a return to the dear old farm, where there was a family almost rapturously fond of life, yearning to know, to do, and to help.

Her heart was so filled with the love of those with whom she had learned the real meaning of life that all newer lovers, of whom there were many, met a firm rebuff, until she had reached the age of thirty-two. June 2, 1880, she married William Henry Greeley, and they settled in Lexington. Then followed nine years of domestic happiness, cut short by the husband's death, December 22, 1889.

In the scant score of years remaining to her, nearly half of which were passed in the valley of the shadow of death, every day was filled to overflowing with life. At first the interests of her growing children absorbed her energies; but, when they had become engrossed in college courses, she applied herself to the service of the community.

A vigorous, original thinker, as well as a wide reader and careful student, she was especially interested in the study of the Bible, and in her later years became a well-known apostle of its modern interpretation. Her clear expositions of the old Hebrew character, and the helpful applications which she made of its teachings to present-day problems, will long be remembered by those who were members of her class in the Sunday-school of the First Parish (Unitarian) Church. She was called to read her essays on Biblical subjects in many parts of Massachusetts, and, while physical strength permitted, she gladly responded. Toward the end, though almost conquered by great suffering, she yet said cheerily: "If I only could get well! I have worked out so much more in my mind, and something much better than what I have done before."

The ghastly theology which pervaded the sermons to which she listened in her youthful days left a permanent trace of pessimism upon the girl's mind, but it did not impair the worth of an intensely religious and naturally optimistic nature. Though she reverenced always the church of her childhood, she discarded its doctrines for a broader and more liberal religion. She was ever a searcher after truth rather than one who feels that it has been attained, and is thereby satisfied. Her Puritan love of justice and righteousness, coupled with strong common sense, guided her through difficult ways; and she chose unhesitatingly those things in life which seemed best worth living for. Though a genial and faithful member of this Historical Society, attending nearly every meeting, she valued rather the stimulus which it brings to contemporary life than any merely antiquarian interests which it serves.

A rugged independence, strong convictions, courageously expressed, and a simple, direct manner, which had sometimes a touch not of vanity, but of seeming intolerance, made her some enemies as well as many friends. No one of us can ever forget her exuberant sense of humor and hearty laughter, which brightened and cheered any company in which she was found; and every one who knew her must testify to the fact that a sweet and wholesome influence flowed from her life into the hearts of all with whom she was associated.

Of the disease that was to bring so much suffering, and was in time to prove fatal, she was herself aware long before she permitted its presence to be known by her family or friends. Under its depressing influence she maintained a fortitude not surpassed in the lives of any of the old Hebrew characters which she had so faithfully studied; and through the pain and anxiety with which the closing years of this useful life were clouded the same keenness of intellect and ready play of wit that had illumined life's journey for herself and others, during the days of her health and strength, shone with their accustomed brightness.

R. P. C.

Elizabeth W. Harrington.

1833–1906.

Elizabeth W. Harrington, one of the original members of this society, was born in Lexington, Mass., October 14, 1833, and died in Blois, France, May 16, 1906, at the age of seventy-two years and seven months. She was the youngest and last survivor of nine children, and was of the eighth generation of the Harrington family as recorded in our local history. The first ancestor in this country came from England, and had settled in Watertown as early as 1642. Her father was Nathaniel Harrington, and her mother Clarissa Mead, daughter of Josiah Mead, a former storekeeper at the old store on the site of the new library.

In the third generation we find Robert Harrington, a selectman of Lexington during the Revolutionary period, when much was demanded of public officials. He bore the rank of ensign, and in him Elizabeth W. and Jonathan, the last survivor of the battle of Lexington, had a common ancestor.

In the fourth generation was Daniel, clerk of Captain Parker's company and participant in the events of Lexington's memorable day. He was a stalwart blacksmith and an honored townsman. He married, May 8, 1760, Anna Munroe, daughter of Robert Munroe.

Robert Munroe was born May 4, 1712, was in the French war, and was standard bearer at Louisburg, 1758. He was ensign in Captain Parker's company, and was killed in service on the green at the first blood shed in the Revolution. Another daughter of Robert Munroe—Ruth—married William Tidd, lieutenant of Captain Parker's company.

This in brief illustrates the types of Miss Harrington's ancestors, and explains in a measure, at least, her stanch upright character and patriotic sentiments. She was disposed to original thinking and plain speaking. She was vigorous in mind and body, and showed only slight effects of advancing years.

She was an interested member and willing worker in this society, and her perfect handwriting covers many pages of transcription in our records.

She was a member of the First Parish Church, and a constant attendant at its services.

She was the originator of, and the first to provide endowment for, an old people's home in Lexington, and must always be remembered for this wise and good act, giving rise to permanent organization and incorporation.

She visited Europe about 1886 and again in 1896, and had spent two years in California. She had been in Europe about one year on a third visit abroad, when overcome by sickness and death in 1906.

F. S. P.

CORNELIUS WELLINGTON.

1828–1909.

Cornelius Wellington, son of Peter Wellington, was born in Lexington, May 23, 1828, and died in Lexington, August 27, 1909.

His education was largely in the public schools of the town and the activities of an excellent farm home. As a young man, he worked several years in the dry-goods business, and then went into the lumber business at Stillwater, Mich.

He returned to Boston in 1857, and went into the dry-goods business with his brother, Henry W. Wellington, the firm name being Wellington, Gross & Company, later Wellington Brothers. He continued in the dry-goods business about ten years, when it was closed up, and he joined his brother Charles in the Household Art Company.

About this time he became interested in high-bred Jersey cattle, with which he stocked his farm in Lexington. He went to the Island of Jersey to study the cattle there, and returned with a herd of fifty head. He was particularly successful in dealing in Jersey cattle, and his stock was widely known and highly valued.

He later built a fine residence on Pleasant Street, which he sold to Mrs. Scudder after the death of his brother Charles.

He was a man of strong opinions and undaunted courage, honest, generous, and genial. He was bold in the anti-slavery movement, a member of the Anti-slavery Society from 1845 to the abolition of slavery, a friend and admirer of Theodore Parker, a member of the Free Religious Association, but not a church member and hardly a church sympathizer.

Always interested in whatever pertained to the welfare of Lexington, he was a faithful attendant at town meetings, and he devoted much time to local enterprises of a useful character. For many years he was among the most active and serviceable members of the Field and Garden Club. He was the first tree warden in Lexington, holding the office from 1902 to 1908.

One of the original members of Lexington Historical Society, he remained ever a willing worker for its success and a liberal donor to its archives.

Mr. Wellington believed in cremation, and his body was cremated.

F. S. P.

JAMES SMITH MUNROE.

1824–1910.

James Smith Munroe, the second son and youngest child of Jonas and Abigail Cook (Smith) Munroe, was born in the old Munroe Tavern,* June 6, 1824. His grandfather, William Munroe, was orderly sergeant at

---

* Through the generosity of Mr. Munroe this famous hostelry has lately come into the possession of the society. It accepted the gift as a trust to be administered agreeably to the terms expressed in his will. That instrument declares: "This devise is made upon the express condition that said Historical Society shall keep the premises in good repair and forever maintain the same in substantially their present or original condition, shall pay all taxes and other municipal charges and assessments, if any, which may be levied thereon, shall appoint a suitable custodian to have charge thereof, and shall at stated and suitable times open the house for the inspection of the public. Said Society shall make such reasonable rules and regulations for the care of said Munroe Tavern as it may deem expedient, and shall have the right to charge a reasonable admission fee." A custodian was appointed, and on May 13, 1911, with simple dedicatory ceremonies the main part of the building was opened to the public. Visitors are admitted, without charge, every week-day between the hours of 10 A.M. and 6 P.M.

the battle of Lexington, and was in command of the squad that guarded Hancock and Adams the night before the battle. His father kept the tavern from 1827, when Sergeant Munroe died, until after 1850. For until the opening of the railroad the tavern was an important "last night" stopping-place for a great part of the extensive traffic in live stock and produce coming to Boston from the north.

Among picturesque surroundings Mr. Munroe's boyhood was passed, since he could recall the arrival at the tavern of horses, cattle, and big flocks of sheep, which were sheltered in immense barns back of the tavern. It was part of his work to look after this live stock, and his time and energies must have been fully engaged. Yet he was able besides to earn considerable money by making and selling to the drovers the "snappers" which they used on their whips. Along with this practical training he went to the public schools, and supplemented the mental training they afforded by a course of instruction in the Lexington Academy. After leaving the academy, he went to Boston to work as a sort of apprentice in the well-known shoe store of Mr. John Rogers, a relative, living at Mr. Rogers's house and doing many of the household "chores," besides attending to the work required of him in the store.

Later Mr. Munroe went into the hardware business in Dock Square, in the firm of Sewall & Munroe, and about 1850, through the foreclosure of a mortgage, he undertook for the firm the management of a small paper mill in Bedford, near Burlington, the water power of which was furnished by Vine Brook. At that time the raw material and manufactured product had to be hauled to and from the Lexington railroad station.

When this mill was burned, Mr. Munroe started a larger one on the Merrimack at South Lawrence, and later built the mill now occupied by the Munroe Felt and Paper Company, of which he was for a number of years the president.   For almost sixty years, among other kinds of paper, he furnished a special brand to the New England Felt Roofing Works for the making of their "Beehive" brand of roofing material.

May 23, 1854, James S. Munroe married Alice Bridge, youngest daughter of Elias Phinney (Harvard College, 1801), clerk of the Middlesex Court, and distinguished for his interest in agriculture.   During the first year or two of their married life they lived in the house formerly standing between the Harrington and Gould houses on Elm Avenue.   Afterwards they moved to the "Winthrop" house, almost opposite the Munroe Tavern.   Every tree on their place, except the large elm in front, was planted by Mr. Munroe.   He also converted a large area of swamp land behind the house into an elaborately drained meadow, and did much to beautify the landscape in other ways. Indeed, he had a passion for landscape architecture, and made it his avocation along with general farming and the raising of fine horses, cattle, and swine.

In 1873 he moved to the so-called "Colson" house, where he lived to the end.   His wife died quite suddenly in 1888, leaving three sons: William Robert, born in 1855; John Cummings, born in 1858; and James Phinney, born in 1862.   The eldest son died in 1889, and the second son, who had attained distinction as a surgeon, died only four days before his father.

James S. Munroe never cared to assume public office, although he served faithfully as a member of committees having to do with the welfare of the town, and was active in making the Battle-green into the beautiful place in which our townspeople all delight.   He also brought from the Parker homestead, where it had served for years as a carpenter shop, the old belfry.   For a long time he was influentially active in the Follen Church, especially in connection with the choir.

His house was a centre of simple and delightful hospitality, where he entertained many distinguished persons, and besides gave them pleasure by his enthusiastic guidance through Lexington and its neighborhood. His house was always open to the friends of his three sons, so that it is filled with memories of many hospitable and happy days.

With the exception of one of Mrs. Munroe's brothers, Mr. George B. Phinney, living in Missouri, Mr. Munroe outlived all his generation. Therefore, he was not sorry to go, and after two weeks' illness he died peacefully, December 10, 1910.

Rev. John M. Wilson,
Historian.

PROCEEDINGS.

REGULAR MEETING, February 14, 1905.

Amendments to the By-laws offered by Mr. F. C. Childs at the last meeting were taken from the table and considered. Discussion followed, and no final action was taken.

After reports of committees Rev. DeWitt G. Clark, D.D., read a paper on "Roger Williams, the Puritan Liberal."

ANNUAL MEETING, March 14, 1905.

The usual annual reports were read and accepted. The report of the House Committee showed that 18,057 persons had registered at the Hancock-Clarke House during the year, representing every State in the Union and nearly every country of the earth.

The following officers were elected for the ensuing year:—

President, Edward P. Bliss.

Vice-Presidents, F. C. Childs, Charles G. Kauffman, Charles F. Pierce, Miss Elsie L. Shaw, Miss E. T. Thornton.

Recording Secretary, Irving P. Fox.

Treasurer, L. A. Saville.

Historian, Dr. Fred S. Piper.

Custodian, Miss Marian P. Kirkland.

House Committee, G. O. Whiting, A. C. Washburn, Cornelius Wellington, Miss M. A. Munroe, Mrs. E. B. Lane.

Committee on Publications, E. P. Nichols, A. S. Parsons, Rev. Charles F. Carter, Miss M. E. Hudson, Irving P. Fox.

Committee on Exchange of Publications, Dr. Fred S. Piper, Miss M. A. Munroe, Miss M. E. Hudson.

Corresponding Secretary, Miss M. E. Hudson.

REGULAR MEETING, April 11, 1905.

The President, Mr. E. P. Bliss, spoke on the subject assigned for the evening, "Making History in Lexington," which was followed by discussion. Mr. A. E. Horton read a short paper on Paul Revere's Ride, and said that he had made a map of the route covered by Revere.

REGULAR MEETING, October 10, 1905.

Dr. Piper, as chairman of a committee, reported that a granite marker had been placed on the grave of the British soldier in the old burying-ground.

Rev. Robert W. Wallace of Somerville read a paper on "The Louisiana Purchase."

REGULAR MEETING, December 12, 1905.

The Treasurer, Mr. L. S. Saville, reported the receipt of check for $5,000 from the estate of the late George O. Smith, in payment of legacy mentioned in his will. Dr. Piper read a short sketch, prepared by Miss E. S. Parker, of the history of the store now occupied by G. W. Spaulding, which for many years stood on the site of the new Cary Memorial Library.

The President, Mr. Bliss, gave an address on "The Transmission of History through Words."

REGULAR MEETING, February 13, 1906.

Mr. William Lloyd Garrison read a paper on "The Anti-slavery Movement in Boston."

ANNUAL MEETING, March 13, 1906.

The usual annual reports were made and accepted. The report of the House Committee showed that 12,602 persons, representing 1,359 cities and towns in the United States and 81 foreign cities and towns, had visited the Hancock-Clarke House during the year.

Rev. C. F. Carter, for Committee, exhibited to the meeting a large photograph of the late Rev. Carlton A. Staples, neatly and artistically framed.

The following officers for the ensuing year were elected:—
President, Mr. Edward P. Bliss.
Vice-Presidents, Mr. Frank C. Childs, Rev. Michael J. Owens, Mr. A. Bradford Smith, Miss Amelia M. Mulliken, Miss Carrie F. Fiske.
Recording Secretary, Mr. Irving P. Fox.

Treasurer, Mr. L. A. Saville.

Historian, Dr. Fred S. Piper.

Custodian, Miss Marian P. Kirkland.

Corresponding Secretary, Miss Mary E. Hudson.

House Committee, Mr. George O. Whiting, Mr. A. C. Washburn, Mr. Cornelius Wellington, Miss M. A. Munroe, Mrs. E. B. Lane.

Committee on Publications, Mr. Edward P. Nichols, Mr. Albert S. Parsons, Rev. Charles F. Carter, Miss Mary E. Hudson, Mr. Irving P. Fox.

Committee on Exchange of Publications, Miss Mary E. Hudson, Dr. Fred S. Piper, Miss Marian P. Kirkland.

Mr. M. J. Canavan read a paper entitled "A Spectre seen by Mrs. Weeden at North End, Boston. A Deposition taken down by Cotton Mather."

REGULAR MEETING, April 10, 1906.

No meeting was held because of lack of a quorum.

REGULAR MEETING, October 9, 1906.

Professor Mark H. Liddell read a paper on "The History of English Spelling."

REGULAR MEETING, December 11, 1906.

Rev. Mr. Carter made report of the recent purchase, from the Hancock heirs, of the Smibert portraits of Rev. John Hancock and Madam Hancock.

The Historian read a short biographical sketch of the late Miss Elizabeth W. Harrington, one of the first members of the society.

Rev. John M. Wilson read an interesting paper on William Penn.

REGULAR MEETING, February 12, 1907.

A Committee on the Celebration of April 19 consisting of Mr. H. G. Locke, Captain C. G. Kauffman, and Miss Elizabeth T. Thornton, was appointed by the chair.

Miss Ellen A. Stone read a most interesting paper, consisting largely of extracts from the diary and letters of Miss Caira Robbins, a resident of East Lexington from 1794 to 1881.

ANNUAL MEETING, March 12, 1907.

The usual annual reports were read and accepted. Visitors registered at the Hancock-Clarke House during the year numbered 16,398.

The following officers were elected for the ensuing year:—

President, Mr. George O. Whiting.

Vice-Presidents, Mr. Frank C. Childs, Mr. A. Bradford Smith, Rev. Michael J. Owens, Miss Amelia M. Mulliken, Miss Carrie F. Fiske.

Recording Secretary, Mr. Irving P. Fox.

Treasurer, Mr. Leonard A. Saville.

Historian, Dr. Fred S. Piper.

Custodian, Miss Marian P. Kirkland.

Corresponding Secretary, Miss Mary E. Hudson.

House Committee, Mr. George O. Whiting, Dr. F. S. Piper, Mr. A. C. Washburn, Mr. Cornelius Wellington, Miss M. A. Munroe, Mrs. E. B. Lane.

Committee on Publications, Mr. Edward P. Nichols, Mr. A. S. Parsons, Rev. Charles F. Carter, Miss Mary E. Hudson, Mr. Irving P. Fox.

Committee on Exchange of Publications, Miss Mary E. Hudson, Dr. Fred S. Piper, Miss Marian P. Kirkland.

Committee on 19th of April, Mr. Herbert G. Locke with others.

It was suggested that it might be well, in the near future, for the society to publish a new edition of the History of Lexington.

Mr. A. E. Horton spoke on the bounds of the old Ministerial Lands and the old Town Lands and also of the location of Mount Gilboa.

REGULAR MEETING, October 8, 1907.

Hon. Milton Reed, of Fall River, read a paper on "The Personality of Authors as Revealed in their Works."

REGULAR MEETING, February 11, 1908.

Extracts from an interesting letter, written by Rev. Jonas Clarke's daughter, Betty Clarke, to her niece Mrs. Lucy Ware Allen, April 19, 1841, were read by the Corresponding Secretary.

Mr. James P. Munroe read a valuable paper on Samuel Adams.

ANNUAL MEETING, March 10, 1908.

The usual annual reports were read.

Mr. L. A. Saville, as Treasurer, reported that the society had on hand, in general and trust funds, $16,570, and possessed property to the value of $10,000, making a total of $26,570.

It was voted that an auditor be appointed to verify the accounts of both incoming and outgoing Treasurers.

Voted that the thanks of the society be extended to Mr. Saville for his faithful services as Treasurer over a period of twenty-two years.

The House Committee reported that 15,000 persons had visited the Hancock-Clarke House during the year.

Dr. Piper, for Special Committee appointed to investigate the ownership of the painting "The Dawn of Liberty" hanging in Town Hall, said that there was no doubt the painting belonged to the society.

Amendments to the By-laws regarding membership of the society were recommended to be acted upon at the next meeting.

The following officers for the ensuing year were elected:—

President, Mr. George O. Whiting.

Vice-Presidents, Mr. Frank C. Childs, Rev. Michael J. Owens, Mr. Charles P. Nunn, Miss Gertrude Pierce, Dr. Fred S. Piper.

Recording Secretary, Mr. Irving P. Fox.

Treasurer, Mr. Charles F. Pierce.

Historian, Dr. Fred S. Piper.

Custodian, Miss Marian P. Kirkland.

Corresponding Secretary, Miss Mary E. Hudson.

House Committee, Mr. George O. Whiting, Miss M. A. Munroe, Mrs. E. B. Lane, Mr. James F. Russell, Mr. John N. Morse, Mr. Charles A. Whittemore.

Committee on Publications, Mr. Edward P. Nichols, Rev. Charles F. Carter, Miss Mary E. Hudson, Miss Mabel P. Cook, Mr. Robert P. Clapp.

Committee on Exchanges, Dr. Fred S. Piper, Miss Mary E. Hudson, Miss Marian P. Kirkland.

Committee on 19th of April, Mr. Herbert G. Locke, Mrs. Charles B. Davis, Mr. Francis S. Dane.

Rev. John M. Wilson read a paper on "The Death of Alexander Hamilton."

REGULAR MEETING, April 14, 1908.

Amendments to the By-laws reported at the last meeting were adopted. Among them was one requiring the Treasurer of the Society to give a bond which shall be satisfactory to the Council.

Rev. E. M. Harvey, of Quincy, read a paper upon "Old New England Meeting-houses," illustrated by old photographs and prints.

REGULAR MEETING, October 13, 1908.

The Committee appointed to consider the advisability of publishing a revised History of Lexington reported in favor of such publication, the work to be brought up to date and ready for distribution in the year 1913,—the two hundredth anniversary of the incorporation of the town.

Dr. Fred S. Piper read a very interesting paper called "Architectural Yesterdays in Lexington," illustrated by numerous large and handsome photographs taken by himself.

REGULAR MEETING, December 8, 1908.

Mr. William C. Bates of Cambridge read a paper on "Henry Barnard, a Pioneer in Education: His Works and his Ways."

REGULAR MEETING, February 9, 1909.

Rev. Bradley Gilman read a paper on "The Southern Problem as Seen by Northern Eyes."

ANNUAL MEETING, March 9, 1909.

The usual annual reports were made and accepted. 14,470 persons had visited the Hancock-Clarke House during the year.

The following officers were elected for the ensuing year:—

President, Dr. Fred S. Piper.

Vice-Presidents, Mr. Frank C. Childs, Rev. Michael J. Owens, Mr. Everett M. Mulliken, Miss Gertrude Pierce, Mr. Frank H. Damon.

Recording Secretary, Mr. Irving P. Fox.

Treasurer, Mr. Charles F. Pierce.

Historian, Rev. John M. Wilson.
Custodian, Miss Alice W. Morse.
Corresponding Secretary, Miss Mary E. Hudson.
Auditor, Mr. James E. Crone.
House Committee, Mr. Charles B. Davis, Miss E. A. Robertson,
Mrs. E. B. Lane, Mr. James F. Russell, Mr. John N. Morse, Mr.
C. A. Whittemore.
Committee on Publication, Mr. Robert P. Clapp, Rev. Charles F.
Carter, Miss Mary E. Hudson, Miss Mabel P. Cook, Mr. Henry
H. Putnam.
Committee on Exchanges, Miss Mary E. Hudson, Dr. Fred S.
Piper, Miss Amelia M. Mulliken.
Committee on 19th of April, Mr. Herbert G. Locke, Mrs. Charles
B. Davis, Mr. Francis S. Dane.
Committee on Investment, Mr. George O. Whiting, Mr. Alonzo
E. Locke, Mr. Robert P. Clapp.
Committee on New History of Lexington, Mr. James P. Munroe,
Miss Mary E. Hudson, Rev. Charles F. Carter, Miss S. E. Robinson,
Mr. John N. Morse, Dr. Fred S. Piper, Mr. Albert S. Parsons.
The paper of the evening was by Mr. Roy W. Hatch, entitled
"Foothills of History."

REGULAR MEETING, April 13, 1909.

Dr. Henry W. Piper read a paper on "Forestry."

REGULAR MEETING, October 12, 1909.

Rev. James De Normandie, D.D., read a most interesting paper
on Dr. Edward Everett Hale.

REGULAR MEETING, December 21, 1909.

On motion of Rev. C. F. Carter it was voted that a committee
of three, of which the President should be chairman, should have full
charge of rebuilding the Old Belfry, at the expense of the society,
and on such site as the Committee may select.
Mr. Alexander Starbuck of Waltham, President of the Nantucket
Historical Society, read an exhaustive paper on "Some Interesting
Events leading up to the Battles of Lexington and Concord."

REGULAR MEETING, February 8, 1910.

The society voted to purchase, from the Spatula Publishing Company, the copyright of the Lexington Guide Book, and that an additional sum be appropriated to print a revised edition of the same.

Voted, That a committee of three be appointed on the revision of the By-laws.

Rev. George Hodges, D.D., of the Episcopal Theological School at Cambridge, read an admirable paper upon "The Hanging of Mary Dyer."

ANNUAL MEETING, March 8, 1910.

The usual annual reports were made. The Custodian stated that over 150,000 persons had visited the Hancock-Clarke House since it came into possession of the society.

Various changes in the By-laws were recommended by the Committee.

The following officers were elected for the ensuing year:—

President, Dr. Fred S. Piper.

Vice-Presidents, Mr. Frank H. Damon, Miss Gertrude Pierce, Mr. Howard M. Munroe, Mr. Herbert G. Locke, Miss Mabel P. Cook.

Recording Secretary, Mr. Irving P. Fox.

Treasurer, Mr. John N. Morse.

Historian, Rev. John M. Wilson.

Custodian, Mrs. Ellen B. Lane.

Corresponding Secretary, Miss Mary E. Hudson.

Auditor, Mr. Charles F. Pierce.

House Committee, Mr. Charles B. Davis, Mr. John N. Morse, Mrs. E. B. Lane, Mr. C. A. Whittemore, Mr. James F. Russell, Mrs. C. E. Sprague.

Committee on Publications, Mr. Robert P. Clapp, Miss Mary E. Hudson, Rev. Charles F. Carter, Miss Mabel P. Cook, Mr. Henry H. Putnam.

Committee on Library and Exchange, Dr. Fred S. Piper, Miss Mary E. Hudson, Miss Helen E. Muzzey.

Committee on 19th of April, Mr. Herbert G. Locke, Mrs. Charles B. Davis, Mr. Francis S. Dane.

The paper of the evening was read by Mr. A. E. Horton on "Andrew Jackson Downing, the Father of Landscape Architecture in America."

REGULAR MEETING, April 12, 1910.

Dr. Piper reported that the Committee appointed for the purpose had had the Old Belfry constructed as nearly as possible on its old lines and on the same site.

Rev. John M. Wilson read a paper entitled "New England Witch-craft."

GIFTS.

Framed picture of the Daniel Harrington house, taken down in 1875, and cup made from the wood of said house.

Photograph of Abijah Harrington, son of Daniel. Two Old Farmer's Almanacs, years 1829 and 1832. All given by Miss Elizabeth W. Harrington.

A pocket-book bearing date of 1746 and the initials J. T. O. From Miss Sarah E. Robinson.

Piece of damask from dining-room chair belonging to Dr. Danforth, a celebrated Tory physician of Boston. From Miss E. W. Harrington.

Genealogical Record of Robert Marssey. From Mrs. William Tracy Eustis, Brookline.

Foot-stove belonging to Theodore Parker. From Mr. J. A. Parker.

Old-fashioned vest, dating from 1765. Given by Mr. C. B. Fillibrown, of Boston.

Timbers, beams, nails, and pieces of iron from the Hancock House, Boston. Given by the will of the late Charles French.

Daguerreotype of Jonathan Harrington. Copy of Vicksburg *Daily Citizen*, July, 1863. Donated by Mrs. Alice Bennett.

Piece rug. From Mrs. George H. Reed.

Cartridge-box, originally property of Lexington Artillery Company, organized 1784, disbanded 1847. Roll-call of the Company at two different periods. All given by David A. Tuttle.

List of Soldiers and Sailors in Revolutionary War from the Secretary of State.

Bostonian Society Publications, Vols. 1, 2. From the Society.

Report of Librarian of Congressional Library.

"Bowditch's Navigator," 1849, and Blunt's "Coast Pilot," 1842. From Mrs. Alice D. Goodwin.

Lexington School Registers, 1834-35. From Henry W. Porter.

Ring made of bone by a convict in Charlestown State Prison, and given to S. E. Chandler of Lexington. From Walter T. Ham.

Pamphlet Memorial of Clinton, Mass. From the Clinton Historical Society.

Annals of Iowa. Historical document.

Red cloak worn about 1785 by Sarah (Chandler) Reed. From Miss Emily W. Reed.

Cane belonging to Isaac Bowman 1693. From Miss Clara E. Pleadwell.

Reproduction of Doolittle's "Battle of Lexington." Given by Charles W. Burrows.

Small tray used in Monument House, 1815. From estate of Mrs. Sophia Davis.

Piece of wood from frigate "Constitution." From Mr. Henry Slack.

Piece of wood from Shirley House, Roxbury. From Mrs. F. H. Dunham.

Sword said to have been used in the battle of Lexington.

From the estate of Miss Elizabeth W. Harrington: an iron skillet; a loggerhead used in making flip in Josiah Mead's store; 1 pair gum rubbers; 1 peel or shovel used in removing articles baked in brick oven; 1 hearth shovel; 1 pair wool carders; 1 iron stand; 1 iron broiler; 1 pair steelyards used in Josiah Mead's store; form used in making ladies' caps; also numerous papers.

From Thomas Minns photographic copies of the following portraits by Copley, viz.: Thomas Hancock, from a pastel; Thomas Hancock, from a pastel unfinished; Lydia Henchman Hancock, from a pastel; John Hancock, from a painting.

Bill of Dr. Joseph Fiske for attending wounded British soldiers on April 19, 1775.

Two flags, exact reproductions of the famous Pine Tree Flag and the first American Naval Flag. From Mr. Cornelius Wellington and his sisters.

Records of Lexington Minute Men Association, formed in 1874. From Mr. George O. Davis.

Sketches of the settled ministers of the First Congregational Society in Lexington. From Mr. George O. Davis.

Chair and plate belonging to Jonathan Harrington. From Miss Sarah E. Robinson.

Portraits of Nehemiah and Hannah Stearns Wellington. From Mrs. George O. Davis.

Manuscript sermons and addresses of Rev. C. A. Staples. From Rev. Charles J. Staples.

Numerous deeds and manuscripts relating to Lexington and the Bowman family from Roger W. Montgomery.

An oil painting, nearly life-size, of Colonel William Munroe, orderly sergeant of Captain Parker's Company. From Mrs. Susan D. Smith on behalf of the heirs of Edmund Munroe.

Yardstick formerly belonging to Jonathan Harrington. From Captain C. G. Kauffman.

Commission of Benjamin Reed as captain of the Lexington Artillery Company. From Mr. Hammon Reed.

Autobiography of Hans Christian Andersen. From the Library of Theodore Parker. Presented by Mrs. R. A. Nichols of Roxbury.

Mail-bag used by Postmaster John Davis of Lexington. From Mrs. S. G. Davis of Roxbury.

$50 Confederate note from Mrs. Quincy of Somerville.

From Miss Ellen Stone of East Lexington: a pamphlet, sermons of Rev. L. J. Livermore; anniversary exercises of Dr. Dio Lewis's School for Young Ladies; photograph of the school; photograph of East Lexington (Follen) church; photograph of portrait of Charles Follen by Gambadella; steel engraving of Charles Follen; steel engraving of Mrs. Follen.

Piece of table linen spun by Lucy Munroe Daniels in 1812. From Mrs. C. F. Dibble of New Haven, Conn.

From Mrs. Harriet H. Johnson of Northboro, Mass., letter written by Miss Betty Clarke, April 19, 1841, relating to the battle of Lexington.

Sword used in War of 1812. From Mrs. Quincy Dean.

Miniature copy of Declaration of Independence. From Mrs. George F. Jones.

Fac-simile of Brigade and Division Orders issued to Colonel William Munroe, 1768.

From estate of Miss C. F. Neal: mirror; pewter platter; framed silhouette of Rev. Jonas Clarke; sermons and lists of texts of Rev. Jonas Clarke, used between 1755 and 1805.

Vest worn by Isaac Muzzey of Lexington, 1775. From Mrs. George W. Lane of Arlington.

Cradle used for grandson of Paul Revere. Loaned by Henry D. Piper.

Cradle used by Captain John Parker. From Mrs. Hennessey.

Hand-made plough and pitchfork, date 1764. From Mr. Ira G. Dudley of Berlin, Mass.

Silver spoons, purse, old papers of Revolutionary days. From Miss S. Maria Clarke, Newton Upper Falls.

"The Founder of Mormonism," by I. Woodridge Riley. From Yale University.

Memorial Services in Honor of the late Rev. Alfred Porter Putnam, D.D., President of Danvers Historical Society. From said society.

From estate of the late Rev. E. G. Porter a miniature of Major Pitcairn, autograph letter of Earl Percy, and much correspondence relating to Earl Percy.

MEMBERS

OF THE

LEXINGTON HISTORICAL SOCIETY

1911.

HONORARY MEMBERS.

Adams, Hon. Charles F.
Green, Dr. Samuel A.
Staples, Rev. Charles J.

LIFE MEMBERS.

Clapp, Mr. Robert P.
Parker, Miss Elizabeth S.
Saville, Mr. Leonard A.
Staples, Mrs. Carlton A.
Whitcher, Miss Florence E.

MEMBERS.

Ballard, Rev. and Mrs. George G., Jr.
Batcheller, Mr. W. M.
Bennink, Mr. and Mrs. L. E.
Blinn, Miss Helen.
Bliss, Mr. and Mrs. Edward P.
Blodgett, Mr. Arthur L.
Briggs, Mr. and Mrs. Geo. E.
Brown, Mr. and Mrs. Frank D.
Brown, Mr. and Mrs. Leroy S.
Brown, Mr. and Mrs. Willard D.
Butler, Mr. William A.
Butters, Miss S. L.
Butters, Mrs. Frank V.
Carleton, Miss Gertrude W.
Carter, Rev. and Mrs. Charles F.
Cary, Miss Alice B.
Childs, Mr. and Mrs. Frank C.
Childs, Mr. and Mrs. George H.
Clapham, Mr. Edward G.
Clapp, Mrs. Robert P.
Coburn, Mr. and Mrs. Frank W.
Cook, Miss Mabel P.
Crone, Mr. and Mrs. James E.
Crosby, Mrs. Medora Robbins
Damon, Mr. Frank H.
Dana, Miss Ellen E.
Dane, Mr. and Mrs. Francis S.
Davis, Mr. and Mrs. C. B.
Davis, Mr. and Mrs. George O.

Dean, Mr. and Mrs. Francis W.
Doe, Mr. and Mrs. C. C.
Eaton, Mrs. Louisa K.
Fay, Mr. and Mrs. H. F.
Fay, Miss Helen B.
Fiske, Miss Carrie F.
Fiske, Miss Emma I.
Fitch, Miss Mary A.
Fobes, Mr. and Mrs. E. F.
Fox, Mr. and Mrs. Irving P.
Gilmore, Mr. and Mrs. George L.
Goodwin, Mrs. Alice D.
Goulding, Mr. and Mrs. G. L.
Hamlin, Miss Emma C.
Harrington, Miss Clara W.
Harrington, Miss Ellen E.
Harrington, Miss Martha M.
Herrick, Mr. and Mrs. F. W.
Hill, Mr. and Mrs. Willard C.
Hines, Miss Helen
Hudson, Miss Mary E.
Hunt, Miss Anstiss S.
Hunt, Mrs. E. M.
Hunt, Mr. and Mrs. William
Hutchinson, Mrs. J. F.
Jackson, Mr. and Mrs. George H.
Jackson, Mrs. George S.
Jones, Mrs. George F.
Kauffmann, Mr. Charles G.
Kauffmann, Miss M. Fannie
Kettell, Mr. and Mrs. Charles W.
Kimball, Mr. and Mrs. Frank R.
Kirkland, Miss Marian P.
Knowles, Rev. Samuel
Lane, Mrs. Ellen B.
Locke, Mr. and Mrs. Alonzo E.
Locke, Miss Henrietta M.
Locke, Mr. and Mrs. Herbert G.

Luke, Mr. and Mrs. W. J.
Mackinnon, Miss Barbara
Merriam, Mr. E. P.
Milne, Mr. and Mrs. G. D.
Morse, Mr. and Mrs. John N.
Mulliken, Miss Amelia M.
Mulliken, Mr. E. M.
Mulliken, Mr. and Mrs. John E.A.
Munroe, Miss M. Alice
Munroe, Miss Elmina
Munroe, Mr. Howard M.
Munroe, Mr. and Mrs. James P.
Munroe, Mr. Robert Gookin
Munroe, Mrs. William R.
Muzzey, Miss Helen E.
Muzzey, Miss Susan W.
Nichols, Mr. E. P.
Nunn, Mr. and Mrs. Charles P.
Osgood, Dr. Harry B.
Owens, Rev. Michael J.
Parker, Mr. Charles M.
Parsons, Mr. and Mrs. Albert S.
Peaslee, Mrs. Louise W.
Peirce, Mr. Frank D.
Perkins, Mr. and Mrs. Walter B.
Philbrick, Mr. and Mrs. Eliph-
    alet F.
Pierce, Mr. Alfred
Pierce, Mr. and Mrs. Chas. F.
Pierce, Miss Gertrude
Piper, Dr. Fred S.
Preston, Mr. and Mrs. Elwyn G.
Prince, Mr. and Mrs. James P.
Putnam, Mr. and Mrs. H. H.
Putnam, Mrs. Louise H.
Raymond, Mrs. F. F.
Raymond, Mr. Henry S.
Redman, Mrs. Edith C.

Reed, Mr. and Mrs. George F.
Robertson, Miss Emma A.
Robinson, Miss Frances M.
Robinson, Mrs. F. O.
Robinson, Miss Sarah E.
Rowse, Mr. and Mrs. W. W.
Russell, Mr. and Mrs. James F.
Scott, Hon. and Mrs. A. E.
Seeley, Mr. and Mrs. O. G.
Shannon, Dr. and Mrs. Clarence
Shaw, Miss E. L.
Sherburne, Mr. and Mrs. F. F.
Sherburne, Mrs. Warren
Spaulding, Mr. and Mrs. G. W.
Sprague, Mr. and Mrs. Clarence E.
Stevens, Mr. and Mrs. R. L.
Stickle, Mr. and Mrs. W. C.
Stone, Mr. Edward C.
Streeter, Mr. and Mrs. G. H.
Taylor, Mrs. George W.
Tenney, Mrs. Benjamin F.
Thornton, Miss E. T.
Tilton, Dr. J. O.

Tower, Miss Ellen M.
Tower, Mr. and Mrs. Richard G.
Tyler, Mr. Daniel G.
Tyler, Dr. Winsor M.
Valentine, Dr. and Mrs. H. C.
Van Ness, Mrs. Sarah B.
Washburn, Mr. and Mrs. A. C.
Wellington, Miss Caroline
Wellington, Mr. Herbert L.
Wetherbee, Mr. and Mrs. A. A.
Whiting, Mr. and Mrs. George O.
Whitman, Miss Kate
Whitney, Mr. Arthur C.
Whittemore, Mr. and Mrs. Charles A.
Willard, Mr. and Mrs. J. H.
Wilson, Rev. and Mrs. John M.
Wiswell, Mr. and Mrs. C. H.
Worthen, Mr. Edwin B.
Worthen, Mr. George E.
Wright, Miss Abbie E.
Wright, Miss Emma E.
Young, Mr. and Mrs. Owen D.

NECROLOGY.

Brown, Mr. Benjamin F. . . . . July 5, 1908

Brown, Mrs. Benjamin F. . . . . February 18, 1909

Bryant, Mrs. A. W. . . . . May 11, 1905

Fowle, Mr. Charles A., Jr. . . . . December 7, 1910

Gookin, Mrs. F. S. . . . . February 19, 1911

Greeley, Mrs. H. M. . . . . February 2, 1906

Hamblen, Mrs. Florence D. . . . . July 23, 1908

Harrington, Miss Elizabeth W. . . . . May 16, 1906

Mitchell, Mr. Abbot S. . . . . March 20, 1908

Munroe, Mr. James S. . . . . December 10, 1910

Phinney, Miss Jane . . . . August 20, 1907

Pierce, Mrs. Alfred . . . . April 23, 1910

Reed, Mr. Hammon . . . . May 2, 1911

Reed, Mrs. Hammon . . . . January 6, 1908

Robinson, Mr. Theodore P. . . . . November 2, 1910

Robinson, Mrs. R. Eliza . . . . November 10, 1906

Shaw, Mr. Elijah A. . . . . June 9, 1905

Sherburne, Mr. Warren . . . . April 24, 1907

Smith, Mr. Albert Bradford . . . . June 30, 1910

Thayer, Mrs. Elizabeth F. . . . . August 16, 1907

Wellington, Mr. Cornelius . . . . August 27, 1909

Wellington, Miss Eliza . . . . June 11, 1911

Wellington, Mr. Walter . . . . August 23, 1906

Whitney, Mrs. A. C. . . . . October 10, 1911

www.ingramcontent.com/pod-product-compliance
Lightning Source LLC
Chambersburg PA
CBHW032007060726
47497CB00017B/2375